TIME PIECES

Norwich Forum Writers

TIME PIECES

Norwich Forum Writers

TIME PIECES
First Published in 2019 by Norwich Forum Writers.

© Norwich Forum Writers, 2019.
© Copyright for each story / poem / script is the property of each of the authors.

Printed and bound in England by Biddles Books Ltd.
https://www.biddles.co.uk

ISBN 978-1-913218-21-8

ACKNOWLEDGEMENTS

Norwich Forum Writers would like to thank Norfolk County Council Library Services for their support, especially the Norfolk and Norwich Millennium Library for the use of its facilities and their ongoing help and commitment to our writing group.

https://www.norfolk.gov.uk/libraries

The writers would also like to thank Anthony Rosie for sharing his wealth of literary knowledge and for designing and delivering a comprehensive and varied programme. Heartfelt thanks to Anthony for his generous funding and support for the project.

In addition thanks must go to Lyn McKinney for her wonderful illustrations and cover art, Malcolm and Lilly for the design and production of *Time Pieces* and for our distinctive logo, Caroline Lowton for her expertise in proof-reading and The Forum for hosting the launch event and celebration of *Time Pieces*.

https://www.theforumnorwich.co.uk

Finally, thanks to the editing team of Lyn Hazleton, Gill Wilson, Rupert Mallin, Linda Ford, Shirley Jones, Scott King, Lyn McKinney, Hilary Hanbury and Anthony Rosie. They developed a professional and rigorous critiquing and copy editing process and managed the delivery, publication and launch of *Time Pieces*. Sincere thanks to everyone for their commitment, hard work and unending enthusiasm for the project.

FOREWORD

Anthony Rosie

Time Pieces offers readers fiction and poetry on the theme of Age interpreted in different ways. How does a sense of time change with age? Age is not the preserve of the elderly so how does it impact on people at different life stages? Can time and age be understood in symbolic ways? What can poetry yield when we think about age? These and other questions are explored by contributors to Time Pieces who are members of Norwich Forum Writers based at the Millennium Library, Norwich. Norwich Forum Writers has developed through Norfolk Library Service's commitment to community engagement and specifically to supporting a creative writing initiative that began in 2014.

I became the volunteer co-ordinator in 2015 and we moved from the initial 'write what you want' to a programme based on agreed topics, participants' interests and an emerging and agreed rationale. Norwich Forum Writers grew from 2015 and today there are nearly forty people on the email list. We begin our sessions with brief reviews from people on events they might have visited, films, plays of interest, poetry readings etc. This has helped provide a rich texture for our work and shown what a lively place Norfolk is for writers. I was really pleased when some group members brought up the idea of producing an anthology; a substantial task that would showcase the talents of Norwich Forum Writers. It was important from the outset that we did not make contribution to the anthology a requirement for joining in the activity of Norwich Forum Writers. Today Norwich Forum Writers is a strong entity with a group within it acting as an editorial collective.

Throughout its history Norwich Forum Writers has had a constant brief: it is open to anyone who wishes to join us twice a month on Friday mornings. Attendance is voluntary and no previous experience of creative writing is required. We work with a rationale and programme of activities that ensure we cover different aspects of creative writing. Members, where they wish to do so, take the lead on introducing topics.

Producing an anthology to showcase any creative writing group's work often peters out once the anthology appears. That is not the case at Norwich Forum Writers. Here, a dedicated subgroup has taken on editorial and management responsibility alongside the regular creative writing activity for all who attend Norwich Forum Writers. This will ensure the continuity of the longer term programme and the likely emergence of further anthologies.

So, how do you set up a subgroup that will edit and produce an anthology? Norwich Forum Writers as a collective decided how it wanted to proceed, knowing how much commitment would be required. Group members may not necessarily have extensive publication experience in creative writing, although some do have exactly this background. Between them, members have project management skills, extensive experience in working with others, interests in illustration, design and production, as well as a commitment to writing. It was this combination of skills and interest in writing that has sustained the editorial group. Throughout the eighteen months from first inkling to publication, the editorial group has taken control of the production process, including developing bids for funding and liaising with other creative writing groups; exploring how best to disseminate the work of Norwich Forum Writers.

A collective enterprise such as this works when there is trust between group members. This was shown throughout the reviewing process. Each of the thirty seven pieces has been through an anonymous review, where submitters have received constructive feedback and suggestions from other members of the group, with opportunities to change and develop submissions.

Norwich Forum Writers has an identity, a shared commitment to the rationale and programme and, above all, a desire to encourage writing in a variety of forms for audiences. It has been a pleasure to be the volunteer co-ordinator as Norwich Forum Writers has established itself with its first anthology, hopefully with more to come in the future.

CONTENTS

LA BELLE EPOQUE

Lyn McKinney

In 1910, Paris was a catalyst for every creed, colour and nationality. In our house, five minutes from the Seine, our servants were Turkish, Austrian and Belgian. My father loved to hear their stories, and would spend hours on the courtyard bench, in conversation with them, to the great annoyance of my mother. Papa was of Austrian extraction, a gentle but astute businessman who owned several paper mills. Maman, by contrast, was Parisian born and bred, with the assurance and arrogance that only high-born French women possess.

My sister and I attended the Notre Dame School de Paris, which was run by nuns, and every day we would walk there in our grey and white uniforms. One particular day, we were late home from school, and my mother wanted to have the local gendarmes out looking for us, but my father held her back, saying we'd be back before long. He was right. We had followed a painter to the banks of the Seine, watched him with great interest as he set up his easel, and then he had asked if we would like to have a drawing of ourselves. Both portraits took him barely twenty minutes, and it seemed

11

marvellous to us that he had achieved such good likenesses in that time. When we ran into the courtyard at last, we were clutching the sketches for our parents. Immediately they were taken to adorn my father's study wall, a typical reaction from him. My mother, however, glanced at the drawings and then proceeded to punish us by having our Austrian cook, Cécile, come and meet us at the school gates for the next three weeks.

Living so near the Seine was to have its disadvantages. In late January that year, when we were around fourteen and twelve years old, there was a very heavy storm. The rain fell for several days and nights on Paris, causing the waters to rise eight metres above normal height. Papa decided that we should abandon school for the day, in case of flooding. After breakfast he took his mackintosh and umbrella and walked to the corner of our street to be met with the waters of the River Seine lapping at his feet, some hundred yards from its true watercourse. In the distance he could see tree branches and debris being carried like matchsticks in the maelstrom. The water was encroaching on the Rue de Trousseau with some speed, and it would not be long before it reached the square and our beautiful home.

Turning on his heel, he strode back, summoning our Belgian servant Frédéric and Austrian cook, Cécile. He instructed them to close the iron gates, which afforded some protection, since the lower half was solid iron, and to barricade all our basement windows. We were sent upstairs, to be with Maman, who was horrified at the thought of being surrounded by water and unable to get to the shops. She walked to and fro, her long dress swishing as she went, trying to keep calm, whilst calling for Atil, our Turkish servant. She wanted him to bring all our fine furniture and valuable pieces of art up onto the first floor and, when he tried to explain it was impossible, she shouted at him, calling him useless. Thérèse and I watched all this in fits of giggles from the bottom step of the second floor stairs, never having seen Maman quite so discomfited.

The stormy weather continued all that day, and the next morning we looked out of our large sash windows on the first floor, to see people rowing down the street. The authorities were knocking on all doors in the area. Some of our neighbours, who were elderly or alone, were being carried out in punts, to be transported to relatives on higher ground. We girls just watched everything going on, thinking it all exciting. Around midday, the odorous brown floodwaters began to seep under the gates and across the courtyard. They poured down the outside steps to the basement, and began to fill the cellar where Papa kept his wine. There was nothing he could do, as there were hundreds of bottles laid side by side in racks on long tables. Some had been there for decades. To disturb them now would be to spoil the wine.

Uncle Claude was our first visitor during the flood, and he came by boat. He lived in the Latin quarter of the city, and brought news that the vaults of some of the branches of the Société Générale had suffered enormous damage, He'd heard from a bank official that around sixty safe deposit boxes were lost at the Boulevard St Germain, and all the strong boxes at the Rue de Lyon had gone, as well as the furniture. People had lost millions of francs, and all staff were on the scene, trying to pump out the filthy water. Papa said it was fortunate our own valuables were safe, on higher ground. Uncle Claude told us the sewers and tunnels under the city had become so waterlogged they had overflowed onto the open ground, hence the bad smell. He put his leather boots by the fire to dry out, and spent a long time with Papa sharing a bottle of cognac in his study.

It wasn't until March that the city returned to something like normality. In the meantime city engineers built wooden walkways across the floodwaters, so life could continue until the waters receded. But the Metro remained closed for months, and there was no possible way to use the carriage. Once our supplies had run out, Cécile would go out looking for something to cook. Prices rocketed during that period, and there was no electricity for weeks. Maman was like a caged lioness, unable to continue her hectic social life, and spent her time between making the servants' lives a misery, fussing over Thérèse and me, and complaining to Papa. Fortunately he knew how to handle Maman, telling her she was our mainstay in a crisis and how we couldn't do without her.

In the summer of 1913 I turned sixteen, and Maman decided I should be introduced officially to the world. She instructed all the fashion houses to send representatives to our house with gowns for her perusal, dismissing one after the other for some trifle that was not pleasing to her. I would try on gown after gown, only for her to rap her fan on the sideboard and shake her head over and over. Nothing seemed right, until a young woman by the name of Coco Chanel from a new fashion house was summoned. I immediately took to her well cut and innovative designs, pleading with Maman to agree. In all, we ordered five outfits – two day gowns, a tea gown and two very beautiful ball gowns made from white satin. Maman thought them too modern for her, and contented herself with buying two outrageously expensive hats she could be seen wearing in high society. I was ecstatic, though. Thérèse was envious, and Papa said he looked forward to showing me off.

The ball I was to attend was to be held at the Hotel de Paris, and Maman said the cream of Parisian society would be there, from government ministers and influential business leaders to artists and musicians. We spent all of the previous day preparing; sorting out gloves and shoes, decorations for my hair, and jewellery. Maman and I had decided I should borrow her pearl choker and matching bracelet for the occasion, but Papa had other ideas. He waited until after supper and then produced the most wonderful sapphire necklace for me, saying it brought out the colour of my eyes. It shone like the deepest blue sea against the white gown I was to wear. I had never owned anything so valuable.

On the day of the ball I took a long bath and Cécile came upstairs to dress my dark brown hair. She piled it all up on top, then I dressed and put on my pointed white shoes with their silver buckles, and looked in Maman's long mirror. I couldn't believe it was me. Maman had also instructed a photographer to come to us, just before we left. Monsieur Graves spent a long time under his black cloth, before he finally took the picture – Maman and I sitting, with Papa behind in white tie and tails. The air was full of hair oil and rose petals, as we picked up our silk wraps and took the carriage to the Hotel de Paris.

Even before we arrived, I could hear the sound of orchestral music floating down the street. Carriages were everywhere, as well as the new taxicabs and automobiles, and there was much hooting going on as guests alighted. Inside, Maman and I left our wraps with hotel staff, and walked up the grand staircase with Papa to the entrance to the hotel ballroom. As we stood there waiting to be announced, I gave a gasp of sheer wonderment. I had never seen so much splendour in one room. At one end, a small orchestra was playing a lively tune, to which hundreds of people were dancing. Light from the chandeliers was reflected in precious jewels of every hue in the elegant coiffures and on the gowns of women as they twirled around the dance floor. Around the perimeter, well-born families gossiped and swapped stories, whilst others moved amongst the throng striving to speak to people of influence and power. I spotted a friend from school, similarly attired to myself, and waved one gloved hand to her, before Maman could stop me.

Then we were announced and began our descent into the ballroom itself, where Papa guided us to a table and set about finding some refreshments.

Uncle Claude came over almost immediately, and he and Papa stood on the edge of the throng watching the dancing, and talking. A lady of Maman's acquaintance approached us, her young daughter at her side, and she and Maman spoke animatedly for several minutes before introducing us to each other. Amélie told me she had a brother of seventeen, and that they lived in the Rue Varenne. She indicated to Gérard that he should cross the floor and come and speak to us, which he did, taking care to avoid the dancers. We all chatted politely for a few moments, while the orchestra took a break and, upon its resumption, Gérard asked me to dance. Fortunately, it was a polka, which I had learned at school, and we fairly flew around the dance floor. I had no time to study my partner in detail, but I was aware of his eyes on me. When he bowed and thanked me at the end, I smiled and received a smile in return that lit up his face. He would have lingered, but my father was hovering, as the orchestra struck up 'The Blue Danube'. Papa bowed before me and, taking my hand, asked if he could have the pleasure. We waltzed round the ballroom, he resplendent in his white tie and long coat showing off his elder daughter, I in my long evening gown accompanying a parent I adored.

Later that evening, Maman and I were sitting having some ice cold champagne, and Papa came over with a gentleman whom he introduced as Monsieur Picasso. My father admired his work, and had already bought two of his paintings, which were later found to be valuable, as they were fine examples of Picasso's early Cubist period. I knew nothing of art then, and thought his pictures odd. Maman smiled politely, but you could tell she was not impressed with the Spanish artist. He withdrew, saying he hoped to see us at one of his soirées in Montmartre. Papa drained his glass, and offered his hand to Maman, who nodded briefly.

The orchestra had begun an infectious Viennese waltz and it seemed as if my parents had left aside all disharmony and had become young lovers again. Maman, dressed in deep green velvet with a diamond at her throat, danced like a fleet-footed angel. Papa's eyes never left her, from the moment they took to the dance floor, his tails flying as he steered them through the crowds. Amélie and I watched them from the table. She said to me she wished her parents were more like mine.

Towards the end of the evening, there was a frisson of excitement in the assembled company as the Prime Minister, Monsieur Poincare, was about to arrive, and all the new debutantes were presented to him. He went on to become president the following year, so I was very proud to think I had met such a powerful man.

I danced with two or three other young men during the course of that extraordinary evening, but none had touched my soul like Gérard Métier. When I look back over the years, it's Gérard I remember, gently guiding me, his hand holding mine, as we danced together. Maman, Papa and I left the Hotel de Paris well after midnight, and I fell asleep in the carriage riding home. In the morning, it all seemed like a dream, and, of course, Thérèse wanted all the details.

Amélie and I spent many hours together over the next few months, either at her family home, or in the Rue de Trousseau, and so Gérard and I saw each other often. Fortunately, Maman and Papa liked the Metiers, and I was allowed to visit the Rue Varenne without them, though with a chaperone of course. As the weeks went by, I fell in love with this handsome, caring, capable young man, and I think he with me, but nothing was said. Sometimes I would look up from my cards, or sitting at the piano, to find him looking so affectionately at me, I wanted to burst. Maman guessed of course, but said we should wait, as we were both so young. Little did we know then, we were living in what came to be known as the Belle Epoque, and that everything was soon to change.

The following summer, an Austrian archduke, of whom we had never heard, was assassinated by Serbians. Austria-Hungary immediately declared war on Serbia, backed up by Germany. Papa, who read the more serious papers, said it could all end in terrible conflict. He was of Austrian parentage, and had many relations still living in the Tyrol. But he had taken French citizenship on marrying Maman, and of course was living in France, a fact he hoped would protect him and his family. Cécile was unable to travel home to Austria, or to get word of her family. She and Papa sat up late in the courtyard talking about the 'homeland' which I don't think helped either of them. Maman was beside herself that Papa might be required to report for duty, even though he was well over the age limit. Poor Thérèse never got her 'coming out' ball, as we were at war by the time she turned sixteen.

On August the second, all men between the ages of eighteen and forty eight were called up for mobilization into the army. That meant my darling

Gérard would be going away. He reported at the recruiting centre, then came straight over to us, in his uniform, to say goodbye. I was distraught. Maman fell on him when he arrived, saying he looked so handsome and then burst into tears, saying he would be missed so much. Amélie and I had become close friends by now, and if it had not been for her, I don't think I could have borne what was to come. Papa took him into his study, poured him a cognac, and said we would all be waiting for his return, when he and Gérard could resume their long-standing game of chess.

When it was time for him to leave, Papa made sure Maman was occupied safely in the parlour, before encouraging me to see Gérard out. We sat very close on the courtyard bench, our hands clasped in the evening sun, and he reached out and caressed my cheek with his hand, before kissing me tenderly and whispering, 'Au revoir, mon amour.' Then he got up and walked toward the iron gates, turned briefly as if to record the scene in his mind, and slipped through them. That was the last time I saw him alive. I later heard from an inconsolable Amélie that he'd died in the Battle of the Marne. The chess game with Papa was never finished.

ON BRAZEN STREET

Rupert Mallin

We met
in loud clothes
by a shop which once sold paisley pattern ties
near the Chinese apothecary
on Brazen Street
there to buy wax candles for my ears
and some cream for my eyes.

You said, loudly, 'You look well.'

And then we treated ourselves to cake.
You told me as it arrived, 'Cake!'

Later, you lit my candle
just before I fell asleep.

Too soon I was on my feet
for my ear had caught fire.

'A few blisters but a complete success,'
you shouted, twice.

After a compress
of cucumber, lavender and ice
my life turned into a charade:

through the arctic in my ears
and the garden over my eyes
I saw your semaphore impressions
as you retold the story of my life to me
shouting: 'With a parrot! A parrot!'
and I felt foolish, with nowhere to go

but happiness.

AGELESS LOVE

Shirley Valentine Jones

Although George had been allotted an EazyLivCapsule two years ago, in 2083, he had been lately finding it more and more difficult to look after himself. At the age of one hundred and thirty one it was not easy to always dress himself – even though he had the help of Robert the Robot.

The details of his difficulties are not the most interesting. The usual problems from the self-flushing toilets being too violent, to not really being able to stop his daily soup ration from dribbling all down him when trying to find his own mouth, and therefore having to use the communal clothes washing machines too often. The local street wardens had noticed that. He had tried to keep going on his own in his capsule for as long as possible because he dreaded the next step. His beloved Mary had been forced to live in a commune for the last two years and, on his visits, he knew that she was not happy.

Of course, he only visited her on official visiting days. The NextStepF home opened its doors to visitors every third Sunday of the month. It was much better at arranging that visiting slot than some other end-days-homes. Some didn't allow visitors at all - there had been protests about that on National Protest Day but, as usual, nothing had been changed. So each month George was picked up in the community hover bus and taken to NextStep home, number 1060F, to see Mary. Most times she recognised him and they could always have a little laugh together. After all, they had been married for one hundred and ten years. Their titanium anniversary was coming up fast. He was looking forward to seeing her on the next bus run in three weeks' time on February 27th which happened to be their one hundred and tenth wedding anniversary.

He realised he missed the laughs they used to have more than anything. Mary had been forcibly taken by the authorities from their last home together – a tiny HoverHome – when it became obvious that she could not remember her Personal Insurance Number. They came round and tested her – for more than two hours, he recalled. Asked her basic questions like what year it was, when did England become the fifty third state of USA, who ruled Scotland, who was the governor of the State of England, when was the bridge over the channel built?

Mary had not been managing to run their old RobotHelp either. To activate them you had a finger print pad in conjunction with a code. She couldn't set his buttons in the right order and the house had begun to smell. You just can't cover up smells, so when the monthly inspection of council properties happened, they soon found out that Mary had big problems. George had done his best to help, but he had no access to Robert's code. Only Mary was told the code through her ear-piece when she wanted to start the RobotHelp. Only Mary was designated to use the robot while she was living in their HoverHome. They could have still been together, George thought bitterly, if they both had been allowed to share the responsibilities of running a home. But because of the strange backlash caused by the Women's Power Movement, women had been more tied to the home now than they had been for a century.

George didn't know for certain why the local sort office set the designation rule. It seemed a harsh one - that only one person in the household should have access to the help of the robot, and that should be the woman, if there was a woman living there. He suspected, though, it might have something to do with their central office having knowledge of whether the person responsible for the house interior was up to the job. It might also be, he thought, so that each robot could last a bit longer than they used to. Money saving – again. After all, each robot cost about $30,000. They were, at one time, coded to be used by anyone in the house, but all the different finger touches and rough handling from the youngsters confused some of the robots and they stopped responding as they should. It had been known, it was whispered, that some RobotHelps had gone berserk and messed up their homes – actually broke things. All those replacement robots would be very expensive. They would have cost millions of dollars. And, of course, the authorities were afraid that, eventually, a robot out of kilter might attack a human. It had been whispered that ...

The other suspicion that George had was that, with one-robot-one-user, the authorities could know immediately if the designated person was well or not. That's how they caught Mary. They knew that her mind was going. Half remembered codes, placing the wrong finger on the recognition pad, her unclear voice responding to the voice instructions. Once a person was known to be a malfunctioning human, the authorities didn't allow them to stay in their HoverHome. So at the age of one hundred and twenty six – two years ago – his Mary had been sent into the nearest female NextStep home. George was, at the same time, sent to live in a capsule.

He knew he would never live with Mary again. Women went into female NextStep homes and men went into male NextStep homes. That had become law in 2043 – at the height of the international sexual predatory concerns. It had become a neat solution for England's Senate House to force local councils to have only male nurses in men only homes, and female only nurses in women's homes. It had certainly been effective – the cases of sexual assault in old people's nursing homes had gone down by 95%. What sort of people were the remaining 5%, wondered George? For couples like them it was a painful and cruel separation, for lawyers a big drop in income for there were far fewer litigations, but for the senators a quick and simple way to bring down the crime figures. The House of Representatives in Washington had watched those crime statistics in all the fifty three states since guns had been outlawed. It was common knowledge that if the crime figures went up – then guns would be allowed to be sold to the public once again. The remaining problem was with transgender people – of whom there were now many. The senate was debating whether to open transgender NextStep homes in each state county to take care of that problem. But who would nurse them? George thought that was a step too far – but never said so in public. Ponderings like these flooded into George's mind sometimes. He knew he questioned too much.

The same with schools. For years it had been single sex schools, girls taught by women teachers and boys by men teachers. Sensible really, thought George. Put everyone out of temptation's way. But on the other hand, thought George, mental health problems with the young had tripled in the last ten years. He could not remember, in the 1960s, any case of his school mates having had mental health problems. It was strange that it was so prevalent now. Instability of families, he thought. Lack of father figures, lack of mother figures too, I suppose, he pondered.

On looking down at his forearm, George was suddenly reminded of their wedding day in 1977. They had chosen 'A Whiter Shade of Pale' as their going-down-the-aisle music. Both of them loved Bach and both of them admired Procol Harum's arrangement. George smiled as he looked down - his poor forearm was certainly a whiter shade of pale now, except for all those veins ... He now had his old father's arms, he mused. Better not have that music played at his extinction! He shuddered – he knew he wasn't coping very well on his own.

Mary and he had met at the local Battersea Saturday evening dance. He had never been much of a dancer but it was a good place to meet girls. The dances were at the town hall at the Latchmere. He remembered that the boys all stood at one end of the ball room and the girls at the other. It was a matter of the meeting of the eyes.

At the end of the evening, whomever you had the last dance with, you could accompany home. It took George two months to pluck up courage to ask Mary for the last dance and he then found that the way she nestled into his body meant she would let him see her home.

The evening almost ended in disaster though. They had wandered along the streets, stopping in doorways for a kiss, finding endless things to talk about – it was as if the words had been just waiting to be heard – the ideas to find a real home – above all, they made each other laugh. But all this took a long time – they had left the dance hall at 11 pm and by the time Mary had reached the end of her road it was nearly 2 am. Of course, in those days, neither of them had a watch or a mobile phone – watches unaffordable and mobile phones not invented.

Mary's mother met them and shouted at them both, 'Where have you been?' George had muttered something and then walked away, feeling awkward but hoping that he would meet Mary again. He felt comfortable with her – there were no pretensions. He had continued to feel that all their married life. They had never had children – not for want of trying and wishing. But, if babies didn't happen naturally, neither of them believed in artificial interference.

George got out his meal packet from the freezer and popped it in the jet wave, heated up a carton of tea and then carefully put on his tea-towel bib. He knew he mustn't dribble down himself again after that sudden ear-phone message telling him he was using the community washing machine much too often. One thing the authorities did not know was that he could have been using the washing machine much more if he didn't wash his pyjamas from time to time - when he was having a shower. They sometimes got a little wet during the night. Nothing much, but ...

It only took two months before the authorities came knocking on George's door. 'We need to test you in depth' they said. He knew exactly what that meant. He quickly reminded himself – when he was born, what his first school was called, what was the date of his marriage? Where did he move to after Battersea? What was the make of his first car? What was it powered by? Could he give his robot's code to them? When they did question him, it went on for about an hour and a half – too long, felt George, exhausted by the end of the session. He had no idea how well he had done. He tried to read their expressions - but they gave nothing away.

One week later, the message came through his television that he had failed the test and arrangements were being made for him to 'live a safe life' in a NextStep Home 2013M. He felt a moment of real panic but then thought to himself that Mary had gone through this, and anyway this was a way of sharing something of his life with her. They would be in the same boat, he smiled to himself.

George began to clear out unnecessary clutter – there wasn't all that much since the move from HoverHome to EazyLiv Capsule – but it was surprising how much new stuff he had collected. He found it hard to detach himself from Robert the Robot. Robert had become so much part of his life – and indeed his nearest companion. Not cuddly – certainly – but always ready and always there. His speech was limited but at least they had some sort of bland conversation, often about the weather. After a couple of decades of continental warmth, England had reverted to her type and was now back to unpredictable weather patterns and, what George called, 'proper' seasons. Water was in short supply, though.

The day came. George was ready: prepared inwardly, but raw-weeping inside that he would not be able to visit Mary ever again. There were no community HoverBuses between NextStep homes now – not since a few couples had met and tried to escape – to be together again somehow.

The men knocked at his door early that morning. George had stood Robert by the door so they could 'see' each other for the very last time. It is quite difficult to understand the bond they had between them. But it felt very real to George.

The two men put George in the back of the AmbiBus and made cheerful remarks to him. George had of course been thinking of Mary and had wondered if he could ask them to do something special for him. They seemed so friendly that, before they shut the doors, he plucked up courage to ask them.

'Excuse me,' he said 'I hope you don't mind me asking and I'm quite ready for you to say no.' They interrupted in a jolly way saying 'Oh – go on – ask – you'd be surprised what we can do.' Encouraged, George outlined his plan. 'Could you,' he hesitated. 'Might you be able to just take me first to see my wife Mary in her NextStep? I won't ever be seeing her again and we've been married for 110 years.' With that, the AmbiBus paramedics looked at each other and decided at least they could contact their boss and ask him if they could make a quick detour. With George listening, they spoke to their boss in their control office and put George's request to him. There was a silence, then an 'OK. But don't spend more than three quarters of an hour. It's St Valentine's Day – so it's a special yes,' the boss said. George was one huge smile as they hovered above the houses. On arrival at NextStepHome1060F, the AmbiBus paras had a brief conversation with the home's director who was willing to let George and Mary be together for twenty minutes.

They spent most of the time hugging each other with not too much conversation but a lot of understanding. At the end of the time together Mary handed George her old spectacle case. He looked down at it and wondered why she gave him such a strange keepsake. She was wearing her glasses – so it must be empty. I suppose, he thought, that's really what we've come down to. Our presents to each other have to be our old spectacle cases! There were some tears, some last minutes kisses and then they had to part. They looked at each other for as long as they could as George was led out of the room – and back to the AmbiBus.

At NextStepHome2013M he was settled into his tiny room. After tea he was alone and he took out Mary's spectacle case to see if there was anything in it. It was brown, battered and very ordinary. He opened it and there, on top of a heap of pills, was a short note in Mary's very shaky handwriting. 'Let's go together February 27th. Love you.' George understood immediately what Mary wanted. She must have been collecting her sleeping pills over the last few months. In this year of 2085, they were to die together as they had lived together - loving each other, he hoped, forever.

The Huff Puff Bird

Simon Richardson

At first the tide and sharp
pull of a man
(it seemed to her)
a lover, protector,
his open hand
on her life.
Time dulls the living statue
softens its perfection.
She, the daily wife,
expected the beautiful forever.

His shape changes,
he watches from the mirror
his bearded stoop,
the truth cannot lie,
he is no longer the mover
of worlds. He flaps by her side,
ambles in gliding age
dodo, flightless man.

He settles, relaxes, nests
among his votive choices,
in love with her
and his favourite chair
choosing to roost.
The huff puff bird.
At night, unmoving,
she listens to the man raven
and thinks 'nevermore',
each soft caw and grunt
of a sleeping feathered thing.

Darkening strange music
alters him: this bird fell from
paradise,
his claws rest like prayer on
the linen throw, beaked, lippy,
open to the moon. She
wonders if he will learn to fly
or migrate in symmetry
duck walk, a half thing, loon,
the huff puff bird.

FOR COURAGE

Gill Wilson

In the faded photograph of my father's grave stood a young woman that I didn't recognise. She was wearing a dark coat and a woollen scarf wrapped tightly around her neck. In her hand was a humble posy of cornflowers which she was placing on the fresh mound of earth. Turning the picture over, I read the inscription: 'Monique, 1948'. Fifty two years ago. The handwriting was unfamiliar. It was not my mother's. Who was this girl? What was her connection to my father?

At the head of the grave was a wooden cross with my father's name, Kenneth Davidson, followed by the letters DFM. I knew this referred to the medal he was given for bravery.

I remembered the day, after the landings in Normandy in 1944, we went to Buckingham Palace to collect my father's award from the king.

'Up you go Eddie.' He lifts me up while a man takes a picture of us for the newspaper. The palace is bigger than I expected. It's very busy with lots of other people who have also come to collect their awards. When my father steps forward, the king shakes his hand and says something to him but Dad won't tell

me what he said. Tomorrow he is coming with me to school so that he can tell my classmates all about it in assembly. Everyone will want to ask me about my day in London. I feel like I'm a hero too.

Back home he nearly goes and spoils it. He puts the medal away in a drawer, saying to Mum that he has not done anything special. 'No more than all of the others,' he says. She tells him not to be so modest. He is a hero as far as she is concerned.

It was later that same year that, like many other aircrew, my father had been declared missing, presumed dead. I always assumed that what remained of him had been gradually consumed in secret silence by the local countryside wherever his aircraft had crashed, leaving little to show for his all too brief sojourn into this world.

I climbed into the attic to investigate the contents of my father's old blue trunk, hoping it would provide answers to my many questions. It had his name stencilled in white on the lid and had remained untouched for at least the twenty five years since my mother had died in 1975. I would not be opening it now if not for the letter I had received from a man called Vic, telling me that he had known my father well. He asked if we could meet and gave me his phone number. I don't remember my father mentioning his name but then he didn't talk much about the war when he was home, and I was very young. But curiosity got the better of me and I made the call. Would I be pleased that I accepted his invitation when I returned home or filled with regret? I just didn't know. It's like one of those puzzles that, once you have taken it apart, you can never put it back together.

As I lifted out his old uniform jacket, I had to catch my breath. The smell of my father's tobacco wafted into the room and I was immediately taken back to the old scullery where I would sit on his knee, sorting through his collection of cigarette cards.

'Eddie, give your dad some peace and quiet now will you?'

'He's all right, Renée. Give the lad a break. I'm off again tomorrow.' He stubs out his cigarette. 'Come on Eddie, give us a hand in the garden.'

In 1945, when the war finally ended, we celebrated along with our neighbours. Those who had also lost loved ones understood the complexity of our feelings of joy, mixed with unbearable grief. For the street party that was hastily arranged, my mother wore the miniature gold and blue enamelled pilot's wings my father had given her; and a bright red, lipstick smile.

'If only he'd stuck to training,' she grumbled. 'He'd done his bit. Why volunteer to go back again? It was so nice when he was closer to home.'

It's a beautiful summer's day with a clear, blue sky. An aeroplane flies low over the garden and dips its wing. My mother's face is transformed by a rare, dazzling smile as she looks up. 'Look! It's your father, Eddie. He always comes over the house to say 'hello' when he can.'

Everything changed when the war was over. The cloud under which we had existed became darker, as if filled with heavy rain, rather than showers. Without my father, my mother was a broken woman. She walked with a sense of shame, rather than pride and I couldn't understand what caused her to feel this way. I didn't ask questions for fear that the sadness would suffocate us. There was an unspoken agreement that the subject of my father was best left, and I got little from her over the years. Even his medal, lying in the bottom of the drawer disappeared. It probably went, along with everything else of value, to provide the new pair of shoes, the football kit or the rare Sunday joint. I knew my mother was both angry and upset that she had been left to struggle alone.

Digging down into the bottom of the trunk, I found a pile of letters. Many were typed on thin, fragile paper but one caught my eye. With its cursive script, handwritten on a distinctive blue envelope, the letter appeared as if it had once been scrunched up and then flattened out again. It was written on Christmas Day, the first one after my father died.

25th December 1944

You don't know who I am, do you Mrs Davidson?

Well I'm your Ken's little secret. Are you as dull, dreary and fat as he described you?

He was going to leave you, did you know that? And take your boy with him. He said that you were no longer a fit mother. That you changed after the boy was born. He said that we would make a better family together. And we would have more children, OUR children. He promised me that on our last night together at the Rose and Crown.

I knew your Ken better than you ever did. Did you know he could not hold his drink? He caused his own death. He deserved what he got, and so do you. The stupid man had been drinking with the rest of them in the Mess on the day he died. He thought he was too smart to die. Well he got that

33

wrong didn't he?

Every time people tell you that Ken was a hero – you will know that he wasn't. He was a two-timing drunk who left both of us and I hate him for that.

When you wear that poppy it won't be with pride. It'll be no good you standing at the memorial with all them other widows. They will see it in your face. They won't be taken in, not even if you flash that bloody medal around.

Nobody else is going to love you or marry you now, not with that brat to look after. *It was not signed.*

*

I arrived at the *Fox and Hounds* filled with anticipation and dread at the thought of meeting Vic. After discovering the letter, I nearly cancelled, finally understanding the overwhelming shame that had consumed my mother – but here I was. He looked very much as I expected - a typical RAF type. He was wearing an open-necked shirt and corduroy trousers. A tall man, once very upright, he stooped slightly now that he was nearly eighty.

'So nice to see you Eddie.' He had a firm handshake. 'I hope that "Eddie" is all right. It's what your father always called you.' He continued without waiting for a reply. 'I just had to contact you when I came across his medal up for sale at auction. Apparently it's has been part of someone's collection for the last twenty years or more. Drink?'

I watched him as he walked to the bar. It was easy to imagine him in his smart, blue uniform.

When he returned to the table, he sipped his gin and tonic for a few moments without speaking.

'Your father was a good friend of mine … in-as-much as you could have close friends when you knew that you could lose them at any time.' He looked down, unsure of how blunt he could be without upsetting me. 'He was a good sort, one of the best pilots I ever met. That's why they took him off ops … wanted him to train the sprogs, to give them the greatest chance possible. But he wanted back in. He missed the action … the excitement … his mates on the squadron. He didn't like being away from us,' said Vic.

'So … didn't his drinking habits get in the way? Or is that what you all did to cope?'

'What drinking?' Vic looked astonished. 'Your dad was practically teetotal. Rarely let his guard down. You never knew when you would get the off …

couldn't take the risk.'

I showed him the letter. I felt embarrassed, ashamed. I had never discussed my father with anyone and here I was opening up to a stranger.

'This is rubbish,' he spluttered. 'Have you ever seen a Hawker Tempest? Five tons of guns, rockets and raw power.'

The volume of his voice took me by surprise. I looked around to see if anyone else was listening.

'I saw one once at a museum,' I said. 'It was enormous.'

'If you'd had a few drinks,' he went on as if I hadn't spoken, 'you'd never tame her. She had to be flown by the book. If you made a mistake she was not forgiving. Your father was aware of that. He had a lot of respect for the old girl. We all did.'

Vic went on to tell me that the day my father died the Germans were retreating. As a result of this, the squadron was pushing forward, relocating to a new airfield.

'We were pushing the enemy back … the boys on the ground that is. Gerry didn't play by the rules though. The anti-aircraft gunners were still there. We messed up … didn't realise that they hadn't all left. They peppered us … shells cracking everywhere.' He took a breath and lowered his voice. 'I was on his port side when your father bought it. He got hit by flak and his wing caught fire. He was too low to bail out. He knew that his number was up. Your dad just smiled across at me from the cockpit, with a look of resignation on his face, and saluted. I waved back to say goodbye.'

I welled up with sadness as if this was a recent event. I tried to take in this new information. Since finding the letter I had been convinced that it explained why my mother had been so sad and ashamed. If its contents could not be believed then what about my mother? Did she bear all that pain for nothing? Was she denied the right to be proud of my father?

'That letter …' Vic said. 'I've been thinking. There was a woman … called Molly … or Betty, or something like that. She worked in the tea wagon. A bit over-friendly if you know what I mean … seemed harmless at first. But she wanted a husband and didn't mind whose, so the lads said.' Vic smiled but I felt unable to share the joke. 'She'd done it before … got an obsession about a particular bloke. Sooner or later she would move on when someone else took her fancy. Well, she took rather a shine to your father. He didn't really know how to handle her. He talked a lot about you and your mum, hoping that she would take the hint. It wasn't in his nature to be rude. He felt sorry for her but she took that as encouragement. She went around telling everyone that they were a couple.' Vic paused, taking some peanuts from the packet that I had put on the table with the second round of drinks. 'I'd forgotten all about her. I think she was moved to another camp … for causing too much trouble. She wasn't on the squadron when your father died, I do know that. I suppose it wouldn't have been too hard for her to find your mother's address.'

I shook my head. 'I don't suppose I will ever know for sure. I doubt if my mother ever tried to find out. I think that she just believed it. It would have been hard for her to imagine that a person would lie about something like that.'

'Your dad was the best man that I flew with in my three years. He was trusted and respected by everyone. And he was devoted to your mother and to you. You mustn't believe the nonsense that woman wrote.'

Vic produced an envelope that had been lying on the seat beside him. 'I have a collection of medals awarded to men I served with all those years ago. It's become a bit of a hobby of mine.' Out of the package, he produced a Distinguished Flying Medal which I recognised from its distinctive diagonal striped ribbon. I took it in my hand and looked at the edge. I could see my father's name engraved around it and I felt proud - proud for me, proud for him and proud for my mother.

'I want you to have it,' said Vic.

'No.' I said firmly, handing it back to him. 'It's yours. It belongs with all the other men's medals that you have. What you have given to me today has a far greater value than this could ever have. My mother will have put the money to good use and I have lived all of this time without it. But … Vic … Thank you. I am so pleased to have held it once again.'

This left just one question.

'I found this.' I said, producing the photograph of Monique. 'I wondered if you could shed any light on her.' Vic looked at it for a few seconds, turning it over to read the inscription on the reverse.

'Yes,' he smiled. 'I didn't know her name but I do know who she is. Your father came down behind enemy lines. His aircraft crashed into an orchard that belonged to a local farmer. The people from the village came to see if they could help him but it was clear that there was nothing that they could do. I believe that Monique was the farmer's daughter. She was the one who got to him first, poor girl. They buried your father in the orchard. Then, after the war, like many others, he was reburied by the war graves people, in a nearby military cemetery. I had heard that, over the years, she tended the grave regularly.'

Vic drained his glass. 'I reckon that she and her family could still live in the area. How do you fancy a trip to Belgium?'

It Took an Age

Lyn Hazleton

Donna's in her front garden fixing a puncture on Jack's bike. She looks up and notices the man with the camera is walking down the road. She's seen him before, they've smiled at each other, but never spoken. Before Donna realises what she's doing, she's calling out to him.

'Nice morning for a walk.' She stands up, a breeze catching her light brown hair, blowing it in her eyes. She flicks it away. 'A bit windy though.'

He stops, adjusting the camera strap on his shoulder. 'Morning. Aye, the wind's blowing a bit, that's for sure.' He smiles, hesitates, then takes a couple of steps up the driveway.

A northern accent then. She was right, his walking boots and wax jacket gave it away – she can always spot a newcomer.

'Having fun?' he continues, nodding towards the bike.

'Not exactly, but luckily for Jack I know how to fix a puncture.' The man raises his eyebrows. 'My son. He's off on a bike ride this morning. If I can get this fixed in time.' Donna slips the tyre lever into the back pocket of her jeans and joins him. 'Nice camera you have there. I've got a Nikon, the

D5500. I bought it second hand from the camera shop in town.' Gabbling, being over friendly with him, what is she doing? He's the photographer, not her. Not anymore. She hasn't taken her camera out in months, but how can she with Chris and Jack pulling her apart? But this is an excuse. She knows the real reason – she's lost her motivation, her creativity and direction. It still isn't the complete truth, but it's getting close.

'I'm Donna. Are you a professional photographer?' she says, recognising the model of the expensive zoom lens attached to his camera. It's hooked on to a strap he's wearing across his body. She has a similar lens and uses a body sling too – so much easier for when she's climbing over rocks and scrambling across sand dunes. But it isn't his camera that's holding Donna's attention, it's his hands; honey-brown with fine blond hairs and long fingers with clean, trimmed nails. He raises his camera up for her to see with such tenderness, for a second she imagines his touch on her skin.

'I'm Nick. I'm semi-professional I suppose you'd say. I teach as well. This is a Canon 7D. I like the Nikon but I think Canons handle better – for me anyway, it's a personal choice. I use it for landscapes mostly. What about you? If you own that model of Nikon, you must be in a similar position?'

A landscape photographer? Here? Maybe if he was interested in wildlife or flora and fauna she could see the attraction of using a powerful zoom lens. On the mudflats there's always a plethora of interesting birds in their natural habitat, lizards too in the dunes and at this time of year, the stunning sea lavender attracts burrowing bees and digger wasps. The area afforded the perfect opportunities to explore nature. Landscapes though. Perhaps he meant seascapes? They were her niche, how she became noticed. Her early work, before she met Chris was good, no it was better than good. She was a real photographer then, an artist, she was getting somewhere; she exhibited and sold her prints.

'Oh, me? I play around now, family shots, you know.' She leans toward him to take a closer look at his camera and catches a whiff of something woody, pine maybe? A flush creeps around her neck.

'Mum.'

It's Jack, carrying a plastic bowl, water slopping over the sides.

Donna steps away quickly. 'I'd best get on. I hope you get some good shots.' She smiles up at Nick. His eyes lock onto hers, nut brown, soulful. She wants to stay exactly where she is. She senses a movement, but he holds her gaze. Time expands. His hand hovers between them, then he lifts it and runs his fingers through his hair.

'I will, thanks. Good luck with the puncture. It was nice to meet you.'

He blinks and turns away from her. She feels an urge to say something, to keep him close, but she loses her chance. He strolls away. Can he feel her watching him? He crosses over to the esplanade, raises his camera to his eye. The small boats lying on their sides on the mudflats – are they the focus of his composition? She checks the horizon, the sun is too high now, the light too harsh, there's no contrast; he's already lost the warm colours, the dusty apricot hues and the soft pink-peaches. She doubts the shot will work.

'Mum!' Jack is cross with her. She checks her watch and rolling up her sleeves asks him to hold the bowl of water steady.

'Best I get on and get this fixed then if you're going to make your bike ride.'

It takes a long time, but Donna fixes the puncture for Jack. She gives him an apple and a box of raisins, then wags a pointed finger in front of his face.

'I want you back home, bike put away, hands washed in time for lunch. One o'clock. No later. OK?'

'Yes Mum.'

With a couple of hours to herself, knowing Chris won't be back from his squash game until midday at the earliest, she makes herself a coffee. She logs onto her laptop and brings up her website – DMP Photography. She's not looked at it for months, a year maybe since giving up her space in the gallery. With Chris constantly pressurising her to get a proper job, she's not bothered maintaining it. There's no point, especially now she's working in the local supermarket.

She sips her coffee, a fuzzy feeling enveloping her as she scrolls through her seascapes. Was this really her work? The imaginative compositions, the colours, the light. These were her images, her felt emotions. She shakes her head, was she really this good? These shots were taken over ten years ago, yet she remembers setting up every one.

The mudflats were stunning in the early morning when the light was soft. Donna never tired of trying to capture the mood, the delicate balance of water sparkle and intricate shapes made by the tide on the impacted sand. Before they had Jack, if the tide was fully out, she used to walk way beyond the boats, leaving Chris in bed. A weak winter sun at dawn was when she captured her best shots, the ones she was most proud of, taken when she lay prone, propped up on her elbows. She was beginning to gain a local following, even getting the odd commission. Then she fell pregnant and everything changed.

'Marry me?' Chris said when she told him she was pregnant. He was leaning over her, sand sprinkling in her face, his ink-blue eyes searching hers. She felt a twist in her tummy. Do I have to? A frown nipped her brow and she ran her tongue over her lips, tasting the salt on her skin.

Donna blows out her breath. She sips her coffee and continues scrolling. She's printed some of these images, she's certain. She ought to get her portfolio out. Maybe she can show Nick some of her work. She shakes off the thought and takes another sip. Nick, Nick who? She types: Nick, photographer, Old Leigh, into the search engine. Bingo!

His website is understated, minimal text with nothing personal about him, aside from a comment about his work being shaped by his upbringing living in the Lake District. All his photographs are in mono. They draw her in. He's used trees or angles of hills and mountains in his compositions as leading lines to the subject of interest; a V in a valley, a spark of light on a lake. Clever. His study of the rock formations, crags and gullies in varied weather conditions – they suit mono, there's no doubt, the images are dramatic, atmospheric. They tell a story.

She stretches her arms above her head, stands up and moves to the kitchen window. The sun is high, the sea a cerulean-blue mirror to the sky and on the horizon where they meet, a long streak of violet. What is he doing in the flatlands of Essex if he loves the hills? As she ponders the question, Chris's car turns into the driveway. Her hand flies to touch her neck. She snaps the lid of her laptop shut, needs time to think. She runs the tap, filling the washing-up bowl. The front door bangs.

Chris comes into the kitchen. She keeps her back to him. His keys drop onto the table. Nothing … no hello … no mention of Jack or the puncture. The fridge door opens. She clatters the dishes into the bowl and spins around to face him. He's holding the orange juice carton. He's red in the face, sweat marks circle his underarms.

'What? What have I done now?'

'It's what you haven't done Chris.'

'What? Give us a clue.'

'Jack's puncture. You didn't fix it.'

'I didn't know he had a puncture.'

'Jack said he asked you to fix it last weekend.'

'Oh, yeah. I forgot.'

'Is that all you can say? What about sorry, or how did it go, or did I manage to fix it all right?'

'Sorry. How did it go, did you manage to fix it all right?'

'Yes, but it took an age.' She picks up her mug and bangs it down on the draining board.

Chris pours himself a glass of juice, slow and casual, and leaves the kitchen. Donna bubbles up then, flies at him, she can't stop herself, finds she doesn't want to.

'Don't turn away from me.' She follows him into the hallway, shouts at his back as he stomps up the stairs. 'Why can't you do more with Jack? Last weekend, he asked you to go for a bike ride with him, but you said you were too busy. Then the puncture. You could have fixed it in the week and gone out with him today, but you didn't remember, did you? Or couldn't be bothered. It's all about you, isn't it Chris? All the time. Your squash club, your mates, your car.' Donna grabs hold of the banister, leans forward and yells up at him. 'What about Jack!?'

'OK, OK, you've made your point. I'm sorry. Leave it will you, I'll speak to Jack later, make it up to him. All right?' Chris turns around at the top of the stairs and glares down at her, but Donna's already walking back into the kitchen.

She slams the door behind her, walks to the sink and sees Jack coming back from his bike ride. The side door opens and he breezes in. His fringe is slick against his forehead. He tells her he's starving. She drops a kiss on the top of his head.

'Go and get washed,' she ruffles his hair, 'and see Dad. He's upstairs taking a shower. Tell him lunch will be in ten minutes.' As she watches him skip off, hears him thunder up the stairs, an idea comes to her.

It is nearly high tide. The sea, a calm graphite wash, is flecked with orange highlights from the setting sun. The small boats, held fast by their moorings, bob on the water close to shore. Further out into the estuary, where the sea kisses the sky, trails of smoke drift from the oil refinery framing the view. A woman in a red anorak and matching wellington boots is walking a dog. Donna brings up the menu on her Nikon and selects mono. She raises the camera to her eye. She's seen the composition she wants, now is the moment. She presses the shutter.

TEN BELLS
A THEATRE SCRIPT

Rupert Mallin

HARRY IS AN ELDERLY CRICKETER.

AS THE PLAY OPENS, HE IS SITTING ON A BENCH – FACING
THE AUDIENCE – IN HIS CRICKET WHITES, WITH HIS BAT,
PADS, HELMET AND GLOVES CLOSE BY. HE LOOKS OUT AT
THE MATCH (HE LOOKS INTO THE AUDIENCE).

CANNED APPLAUSE. HARRY STANDS AND JOINS IN THE
APPLAUSE. A YOUNG CRICKETER, ED, ENTERS FROM THE
AUDIENCE, TAKING OFF HIS GLOVES.

HARRY   Well done.

ED   Was run out by a country mile.

HARRY   Just by a whisker, lad.

ED   Big bloody whiskers, Harry.

HARRY   Oh well. Woods is in next, then it's me.

ED   I shouldn't have called it – shouldn't have.

HARRY   But Ed, you scored ten – ten on your first appearance for the
         seniors club. Good, that is. I was out for a duck, my first game
         for the seniors – out first ball!

ED   Wow.

HARRY   Took me a couple of seasons to climb up through the ranks.
         I was an opener, you know.

ED   Yes – plaque up in your honour in the club house.

HARRY   In the hut?

ED   Yes, the hut.

HARRY   Was in my prime.

ED   Hope I get to open, one day.

HARRY   You will. I followed my father into the club. Now there was talent.

ED   Good, was he?

HARRY   A clockwork run maker was my old man.

ED   Yeah?

HARRY   His life ran like clockwork too. A meticulous man in every way. He was a sign writer by trade.

ED   A sign writer?

HARRY   Before digital, before plastic, he'd paint all the shop signs, pub signs, notices. Once, I helped him paint a big, big clock – 'The Old Clock Bookshop.'

ED   I've seen that. In East Suffolk.

HARRY   Yes, a big clock face with Roman numerals. Ten after ten was the time.

ED   Ten after ten?

HARRY   When clocks ran on clockwork and had pendulums, a clock that wasn't wound up would stop at ten after ten – usually.

ED   How's that?

HARRY   The arms of the clock got stuck in that position. That's why all sign writers painted clocks that had stopped at ten after ten. Look over there – there.

ED   The Ten Bells.

HARRY   My old dad painted that sign. Stands out, eh?

ED   Yes, it does.

CANNED APPLAUSE. HARRY AND ED STAND AND APPLAUD
TOO.

ED   Great cover drive!

HARRY   Woods, was it?

ED   Yes. He's a good player.

HARRY   He is. I'm in next … They pulled me out of the pub to play.
            Was enjoying me dominoes. And a pint. Captain Canning
            pulled me out. Wouldn't have a team without me. Village
            cricket isn't what it used to be.

ED   No, I suppose it isn't.

HARRY   I can still play all the shots, lad.

THROUGH THE FOLLOWING HARRY SHOWS ED HIS
STROKES.

            The hook … The sweep … The square cut … That little
            tickle down the offside … And the big slog out of the ground!

CANNED APPLAUSE.

ED   Harry, you're in next.

HARRY   Next?

ED   You're in now.

HARRY   Now?

ED   Yes.

HARRY   Now or next?

ED   Now!!

HARRY   Oh! How many runs to win?

ED   Ten.

HARRY   Ten to win. Perhaps I'll just block? I'll just block.

ED   Get your pads on, Harry.

HARRY   Is Woods still in?

ED   No, Woods is out. Canning is at the crease.

HARRY   Oh dear, Canning …

ED   He's on 97, so, with you out there, he can make his century!

HARRY   A Canning century, well …

ED   Just get your pads on! Harry!

THROUGH THE FOLLOWING, ED ATTEMPTS TO HELP
HARRY PUT ON HIS PADS, HELMET AND GLOVES.

HARRY   Canning ran me out once, you know. Deliberately.

ED   Not deliberately —

HARRY   Yes. I mean, we were on the same team. He just didn't like me,
         I suppose …

ED   It's not about liking or disliking. It's all about the team.

HARRY   Yes, well, let's see if Canning's name goes up in the hut again …

ED   Quick, Harry, quick!

HARRY STANDS AS IF TO STEP ONTO THE FIELD BUT HAS FORGOTTEN HIS BAT.

HARRY   Forgot my bat.

ED   Here.

ED HANDS HARRY HIS BAT.

HARRY   You know, I think I need the gents –

ED   Just get out there!

HARRY   Think I do.

ED   Just nerves. You'll be fine in the crease.

HARRY   Nerves? At my age?

ED   Confront them, Harry – get out there!

HARRY   How long will ten runs take?

ED   Not long. Remember, just block.
HARRY   Block, block.

ED   And if they're wide of the mark, let them go.

HARRY   Let them go …

HARRY WALKS TOWARDS THE PITCH. THERE IS A HUGE

CHEER AND LOUD APPLAUSE.

HARRY   Ah, my reputation goes before me! See, Ed?

ED   No, Harry, no – you've been timed out!

HARRY   Timed out!! What the hell is that?!

ED   It's in the rules: you didn't get on the pitch fast enough.

HARRY   What do you mean, lad?

ED   You have to be at the crease within three minutes after a wicket falls …

HARRY   Never seen that before!

ED   In the rules!

HARRY   Ridiculous!

ED   We've lost the bloody match.

HARRY   Oh dear. How many short?

ED   Ten runs.

HARRY   Quite a close game then?

ED   We should have bloody won it Harry!

ED EXITS.

HARRY LOOKS AT HIS WATCH AND TAKES OFF PADS, ETC.
WITH SPEED.

HARRY   Of course, clocks can stop at any old time. Ten-past-ten is just a myth. But it's what my old man told me ...

Canning, Woods, Young Ed and the entire team are gathering in The Hut for some beers and to chew over the mud of my name.

But I reckon my pint is already being pulled over at the Ten Bells. She waved at me, she did – from over the green at the Ten Bells.

Sheila's the best barmaid around. Takes on as many shifts there as she can. Gets her away from her big-head husband, Geoffrey – Captain of the seniors' cricket team, Captain Canning, three short of his century ...

HARRY SMILES.

BLACKOUT. END.

Dad's Big Idea

Linda Ford

I saw it first below the car park. It was surrounded by old sleepers, rusted rails and a pile of discarded industrial machinery, unrecognizable now. The roof was covered in stones. Branches, and a thick carpet of old leaves, were slowly beginning to engulf it. Weeds and nettles grew tall around and between the once shiny metal wheels, now brown flecked and still. Could this be the carriage Dad had been talking about on our last visit to the National Transport Museum and the inspiration for his *Big Idea?*

His working life had been spent on the railway, first as a fireman on the plate of a huge, snorting black steam train until the dust and heat had him gasping for breath and he was forced to train as a guard. 'It was the best thing that ever happened to me,' he told me. 'Not that I thought so at the time. I was desperate to be a train driver. It was my dream. I was shattered when I was told I had to leave the plate or die early.' But it was as a guard he met the people whose tragedies and joys, mixed with the comical, stayed with him and became the wonderful stories I heard when I was a little girl.

I had to have a look.

Climbing through the broken wire fence, I started to scramble down the steep bank, nettles stinging my legs. But the slope was much deeper than it looked from the car park. The brambles and trees were dense and tore at my clothes. I almost slipped. Grabbing hold of a small branch, I slid down; mud and leaves flying up in my face. At last I stopped. I had reached the bottom. Standing up slowly, I checked legs and arms; nothing broken, thank goodness. The forest of overhanging trees and bushes created a darkness and gloom which confused me. Where was it? Had I missed it?

Sitting down on an old junction box, rubbing my legs with dock leaves, I began to think that this was a mistake. There was no sign of a carriage. What had I been thinking? Here I was, at the bottom of a steep bank with no way of getting back up that I could see, and on British Rail property. Was it private? I was sure I was somewhere I was not supposed to be, I could even be breaking the law, not to mention risking life and limb being there, so close to a busy main electric line. I stood up and looked around, trying to decide the quickest and safest way back to the car park. Frustrated, I turned and there it was. The carriage. Deep in the shadows, half hidden by the trees I had seen from above.

Picking my way carefully towards the back, I saw a gap where the bottom of the door should have been. For a moment I hesitated, tried to see through a broken window but it was no good. I had to get inside. One big pull and the door came open, hanging precariously on one hinge. Gingerly, I climbed up and stood at the start of a corridor. It was just as Dad had described it but the once lush, dark crimson seats were showing their age. They were faded and worn shiny from years of passengers sitting, even standing, on them as they reached for their luggage. The string luggage racks, tattered now, hung like torn string bags waving forlornly in the draught from the broken window.

A train shot by. Modern, sleek, like silvery-blue lightning. The carriage just rocked and shook a little and then settled back; silent and still, like an old lady dozing in her garden chair. As I looked at the ruins of time, the clouds of dust danced and floated in the light, creating a haze that merged with the shadows. I closed my eyes and breathed in the scent of age. This had been Dad's favourite place; a place where he had tasted triumph and fame.

Here, his stories seemed so real. A kaleidoscope of images and sounds rolled forward like single frame pictures, then slowed to a halt and I found myself back in 1941, with Dad, moving down the carriage listening to the noise of children shouting, 'Are we there yet?' City gentlemen, in dark suits and bowler hats, looked up from their Financial Times and checked their pocket watches as we walked by. In the next compartment, students, with overflowing back packs, scrabbled through their pockets for tickets while a young couple, hand in hand, smiling shyly at each other, dusted newspaper confetti from their clothes. Further down the corridor we were stopped by a pile of heavy kitbags. Dad shook his head.

'Move these lads, you can't keep them here, they're blocking the corridor,' he said, staring at a group of soldiers, smoking their roll ups, standing next to a window with a poster which shouted: YOUR COUNTRY NEEDS YOU. Suddenly I heard the whine of the siren and the beginning of a distant, steady drone. Fingers of light flashed past the windows. With an ear splitting scream of metal on metal the carriage shuddered to a halt and then, enveloped in smoke and steam, clawed its way backwards into the siding. My fingers went white as I gripped the back of a seat.

Inside, in the darkness, everyone held their breath. The soldiers stood ready but helpless. A mother anxiously watched her baby, thankfully silent, asleep deep in his pram ... a whispered prayer ... The commotion outside overwhelmed the carriage as it rocked and swayed in the barrage all around it. Then, slowly, the noise faded, the carriage settled back. Tensions began to relax. As the siren wailed, the soldiers stood down and began to chat. Dad lifted the blinds and with the light, relief followed.

I breathed out heavily and sat down. The images of the air raids had been so vivid. Rubbing my eyes I looked at the faded posters on the walls ... I could hear voices. Definitely voices, and they were getting closer. Oh no! I looked around frantically. Where could I hide? I couldn't let them see me. How could I explain why I was there? Who would believe that a middle aged woman, rather round and clearly unfit, covered in mud stains, scratches and brandishing a bunch of dock leaves, had innocently wandered into the siding? In horror, I pictured the local newspapers and what my sons would say when they read about my exploits.

Quickly, I crouched down. Through the broken window I saw two railway workers in dirty orange high visibility suits and white safety helmets stop at the end of the siding. The taller man, with a thin, pinched faced and downturned mouth looked around. 'We've come too far. I told you five minutes ago that we must have missed it,' he moaned.

He looked at his mate who was a good foot shorter and bursting out of his jacket around the middle. He was studying a map intently, a pencil stuck behind his left ear. He turned and looked back down the line, then at the map again. He held it out, waving it around and repeatedly pointing. 'No … this is the one Sam, I'm sure of it. Come and have a look.' Sam came over. Sighing, he thrust his head towards the map.

'What am I looking at Bert?' his voice was weary.

'This, here … the signal box.' Bert's finger prodded the map. 'The instructions say … two hundred yards past signal box 8642, junction box XV 196753, and siding to the left'. Here's the junction box see …' Bert patted the old box triumphantly. 'Well Sam, I'm right aren't I?'

Sam sucked his uneven teeth. He looked up ahead. 'Well this might be the siding but I don't see no carriage. Do you?' Bert stomped off down the siding. Sam folded his arms. He clearly wasn't going anywhere. From my hiding place I could see Bert getting closer. Suddenly he stopped dead. 'It's here! Sam it's here! I've found it!' he shouted, doing a funny little jig up and down in his work boots, waving his map in the air.

'Bloody hell, I don't believe it.' Sam came pounding towards Bert. They both stood and looked at the old carriage. 'It's great,' said Bert running his hands fondly down its faded sides. 'Look, you can see a bit of the crest.'

'It's a bloody wreck, that's what it is.' Sam kicked at a loose bit of panelling. 'What do they want with it anyway?'

'Dunno. Mr Riley gave me these papers this morning and said we had to find this carriage by the end of today's shift. Top priority. So here we are.' Turning to Sam, he grabbed his arm. 'Hey let's have a look around, maybe inside?' Bert eagerly started to make his way round to the end. I held my breath. I closed my eyes.

'You must be bloody joking, it's taken us ages to find the thing, we've got miles to walk back and I am parched. Let's leave a cone marker, you can put it on your precious map. I need a drink. Anyway it's a death trap and we don't have the right safety equipment. Mr Riley would be really pissed off if we got ourselves injured or … worse.' Turning, he started to stride back down the line. Bert patted the side of the carriage and slowly followed. With a final backward glance, he dropped a red cone on the edge of the siding, took his pencil from behind his ear and scribbled on his map.

'God bless Sam!' I thought, gratefully, but that had been close. It was time to go. Stretching my cramped legs I stood up, took a few photos on my phone and climbed down. I couldn't wait to tell Dad and see his face when I told him he had been right. However, thinking about what Sam and Bert had said made me realise that we might not have as much time as we thought to get his *Big Idea* off the ground. Taking one last photograph, I stroked the side of the carriage and started to walk back down the line. Looking ahead, I could see the trail of broken shrubs and muddy marks I had left, like a scar, down the steep bank. There had to be an easier, less painful way back up to the car park.

Later that night, surrounded by the newspaper debris and scraps left over from a celebratory fish and chip supper, we sat by the fire. His face flushed and his eyes sparkling in the reflections of the flames, Dad drank his Guinness and talked about the carriage. It had been one of four used when the Flying Scotsman had made its record breaking one hundred miles per hour journey from Edinburgh to London in 1934. Dad had been chosen to be the guard on the train, and for months he and William Sporshatt, the driver, and Ralph Webster, the fireman, had been celebrities. They had been interviewed for the radio, and even taken part in a recording for Pathé News. Dad laughed as he remembered sitting in the dark of the cinema, seeing himself standing on the platform, whistle ready, flag in the air, about to wave the train off. He had saved many pictures over the years but sadly had never been able to get a copy of that one moment.

'We do have a problem though Dad,' I said. 'From what Bert was saying Mr Riley, whoever he is, seems to have plans for the carriage. Otherwise why would he want to find it?' Dad looked at me, his face pale. 'You don't think they are going to scrap it, do you?' he said.

'Well I don't know … maybe not but it seems as if they want to do something with it.'

Leaning forward, Dad grasped my hand. 'We can't let that happen, Ellie. We've just found it. It would ruin all our plans.' Standing up, I put my arm around him.

'Don't worry Dad, I'll track down Mr Riley and see what's happening. In the meantime you need to get the good news to your mates at the Weaver Valley Steam Railway and tell them to get started with their fund raising activities.'

'It's a good job you came young lady,' Mr Riley said, his head showing the strands of a comb over as he looked down at his papers. 'It's down to be towed away and broken up next week.'

I never told Dad.

After a whirl of meetings, plans and local television and radio appeals, Dad and I found ourselves in a taxi on our way to the railway station where he would at last see his carriage. I looked at him sitting next to me in his new suit, brightly polished shoes and grey hair, specially cut for the occasion and my eyes welled up. He looked so happy, I was so proud.

'Your mum would have loved this,' he said, his eyes misting over.

'She would have bought a new hat,' I laughed. Mum was famous for her hats, some more suitable than others.

On arriving at the station, we were surprised to see a large crowd. Mr Riley, also resplendent in a new suit and sporting what I could only assume was a toupée, stepped forward and introduced his boss. Mr Donaldson, dressed in Armani, guided us through the crowd and onto platform one where a little dais had been set up with a microphone and surrounded in flowers. Add the crowds and the streams of bunting everywhere and it looked like some sort of summer festival.

'I didn't expect this', whispered Dad. 'You don't think they will want me to make a speech do you?'

'You'll be fine.' I squeezed his hand. 'Just tell them about your *Big Idea*. Anyway Mr Donaldson looks like the sort of man who likes to make speeches,' I said, as he stepped onto the dais. After talking for five minutes, explaining all about the events of the last twelve months, Mr. Donaldson turned to my dad and asked him to step up. For a minute Dad froze as cameras flashed.

'Go on,' I said as I eased him forwards.

'This is the man, ladies and gentlemen, who is responsible for us all being here today. He never gave up believing in his *Big Idea* and we are proud that he was once part of our great railway family. As thanks, we would like to present you, Bob, with this DVD of your record breaking journey on the Flying Scotsman. I am told it contains shots of all the crew. But also a certain young lady,' he looked at me and much to my embarrassment pointed in my direction, 'told us about a particular photograph you dearly wanted. So we are hoping you will accept this on our behalf.' He picked up a large picture frame and turned it round. I could see it showed the image Dad had seen at the cinema so many years ago.

Amid a huge round of applause, his face beaming, Dad took the picture and turned to the crowd. As if on cue, the sound of a train approaching the platform grew louder and a dark green diesel engine came into view. Behind it, battered, broken in places but somehow still resplendent and proud, was Dad's carriage.

The clapping and cheers were deafening. Cameras flashed as reporters and TV crews pushed forward to get a better picture. For a moment I lost Dad amongst the crowds. As they parted a little, I saw him standing transfixed, staring at the carriage, a tear running down his cheek.

Slowly, people moved away to the waiting room area where refreshments were being served and large displays showed the next chapter of events. I left them to read about Dad's *Big Idea*. The renovation of the carriage by the Weaver Valley Stream Railway would start later in the week and, eventually, once it had been restored to its former glory, it would find its final home as their main museum piece, full of pictures and information of that great record-breaking run; a vivid celebration of the great history of steam.

I walked over to him. He had not moved.

'Come on, Dad,' I said, placing my hand on his shoulder, 'let's take a quick look inside, together.'

Ratio

Anasua Sarkar Roy

I close my eyes
The air warms
I breathe in
Rajanigandha flowers
Offerings to my puja dolls
Placed around my Holy Tulsi
Temple of a girl's devotion
To potential energy

The clap of the front letterbox
Sucks my mind back
Into my body
I open my eyes
To the snowy tracks of the postman
Catching my face
Behind net curtains

Cold heaviness returns
As I remember
I am not playing
Anymore
My body and mind have
Grown
Apart
Over the years

I close my eyes
And I hear
The familiar rhythm of
Drumming Dhol players
Beckoning shoulders, arms and legs
Vibrating in every plane of motion
Dancing partner to the sound of beats
Joy expressed
Unconditionally
To kinetic energy

The phone rings
I listen and don't move
My head is spinning
As Earth is to our sun
With relentless orbit
Motion creating time
As moments stick
Then peal away
Pulling me apart
As the cells in my body
Do not replicate
Accurately
My body fragments
My mind restless
Back and forth
Through the space
Between birth and death
This life.

GREAT-AUNT BARBARA'S PARLOUR

Kathryn B Hollingworth

For many people in the United Kingdom, October 31st has associations with witches, broomsticks, ghoulish masks and pumpkins. It is Halloween after all and I can relate to that; but it was also the birthdate of my grandmother Beatrice and her twin sister Barbara in the year 1900.

As I was born in the sixties, I never knew Great-Aunt Barbara in her youth, but I can recall my visits to her home and my conversations with her. She lived in a Derbyshire village, in a rambling old house which, in a way, served as a social hub in the local community and for people of all ages.

Her parlour was a fairly dark room with a low beamed ceiling. I can still recall the scent of rosemary, basil and thyme, which were stored on the upper shelves of her dresser, along with the blue and white crockery. When I was a child my mother and I used to take walks around the village in the cold winter evenings, admiring the stars in the clear, dark sky. We would call in at Aunt Barbara's house for a chat. There was a patterned oil-skin cloth on the table and we would sit around it and drink tea out of dainty china teacups. The room was warm and cozy, with a crackling fire. Pieces of coal would hiss, as they were spat out onto the marble hearth. I would flick through Barbara's copy of Old Moore's Almanac, in an attempt to predict my destiny. My future was unknown and seemed exciting, a blank canvas waiting to be filled, with only the foreground in evidence. It's two-thirds full now, but I don't regret any of it.

Barbara's home was owned by a member of the gentry who had also owned a hall in the village. Barbara's mother and father, Blanche and Thomas, had worked as a valet and cook for their landlord, as well as owning a small farm of their own. The house had once been a 17th century coaching inn. If I close my eyes I can almost hear the rattle of the carriage wheels on the cobblestones outside and the braying of the horses. I can picture the smart coaches drawing into the yard; see the horses' breath steaming in the air and the stable boy leading them into the yard next door, before filling up their stalls with oats and hay. I can picture the landlord serving ale to his thirsty customers, in the taproom, which was later to become Aunt Barbara's parlour.

As children, my friends and I would visit Barbara often. Her house was opposite the church and we would sit in the boughs of the laburnum tree in her front garden, watching the weddings in the church opposite. The teas for the well dressing, a Derbyshire custom, were held there in the summer and the children would assemble in Barbara's front yard, ready to prepare for the maypole dancing which took place in an area known as The Nook.

I called at Barbara's house with my mother one Christmas Eve. The air was frosty and snowflakes fluttered down from the sky. The choir was assembled in the parlour. The singers wore long crimson and white robes and my grandmother and Barbara served them with buns, teacakes, crumpets and tea. I was sent into the dark pantry behind the kitchen to fetch some cakes and milk for Barbara. As I switched on the light, spiders scurried away into the corners. I shivered in the cold, dimly-lit room, with its flagged floor and antique sink. The walls were lined with shelves where Barbara kept her food supplies; butter in a pottery dish, bread, vegetables and pastries.

The house was a meeting place for the church people and for other less Christian activities too. Sometimes Barbara's oldest sister, Aunt Louisa, who lived in Manchester, would visit the village. Louisa was more educated, worldly and sophisticated than Barbara, and she had one gift that we children loved: the art of reading tea leaves. We would gather around in the parlour, as Louisa prophesied our futures by examining the residue of tea leaves in our cups. From the darkened clumps of leaves, she could decipher writing, initials, and tell us of future journeys and events. Whether she told us what she saw or what we wanted to hear is unclear, but her sessions were very popular.

The shelves in the parlour were full of objects from the Victorian age and from the nineteen twenties and thirties. There were old tins labelled with Johnson's Epsom Salts, Nuttall's Mintoes, Oxo cubes and horse brasses hanging from the beams in the ceiling. Halfway down, between a Toby jug and pewter trinket box, stood a black and white photograph of the family shire horses, Sam and Silver, in a metal frame. An old print on the wall depicted children playing the old game of ring-a-ring-a-roses; the girls clad in laced boots and pinafore dresses, the boys wearing braces and flat caps. This rhyme has often been associated with the Great Plague which happened in England in 1665.

Children would visit Barbara often and sit around the table, close to the glowing coal fire which was lit every day, except for the warmest in the summer. Robert and Julia, the children of one of Barbara's neighbours, were frequent visitors. One day they called in when I was enjoying a cup of tea at the house.

'Do you like my new shoes?' they both asked, lifting their feet up towards Barbara in a proud display.

'They're a lovely colour,' said Barbara. 'And they look very comfortable. When did you get them?'

'Yesterday,' said Julia, her mouth crammed full of sweets, which Barbara had given to her. 'We wore them at school today.'

'They're grand.' Barbara turned to me. 'I remember once that your grandmother and I couldn't go to school for several days, because we had no shoes.'

'Why not?' Robert asked, his eyes widening with curiosity. It was almost as if he was hearing a tale from Dickens.

'My mother had no money to buy us shoes,' said Barbara without bitterness, but I sensed a trace of it when she continued speaking. 'I worked in a shoe factory when I left school at thirteen. Your grandmother worked there from six to six every day. It was hard work and I got very tired.'

I nodded, but the sombre atmosphere was soon forgotten as Barbara poured out two sparkling glasses of lemonade for the children and brought out more sweets in their brightly coloured wrappers.

'We're going away to Spain next week,' said Robert. 'Dad says we'll probably fly above here, so we'll wave to you from the plane.'

'I'd love that,' replied Barbara. 'I've never been to Spain. I've never even been to London. I'm not rich, but I do the football pools so maybe one day I will win.'

'Where would you go?' I asked her. 'What would you do if you had lots of money from a big win?'

'I'd go to Buxton and buy fish and chips,' said Barbara.

My mouth twitched a little, but then I realised that she was being serious. She took a baked potato out of the oven next to the fire, holding it carefully with the tongs in her swollen, arthritic hands. Barbara had no electric oven, just a Victorian oven next to the coal fire and a gas stove with a saucepan, and a whistling kettle. As well as having arthritis in her hands, one of her knees was badly swollen; a symptom of housemaid's knee.

'We don't normally go to Spain,' said Julia, as if she was feeling guilty about their foreign holiday. 'We normally go to Scotland, as my dad's from there. His name is Angus.' She took a sip of her lemonade. 'And my mum's name is Sally.'

'I was going to be called Sally,' said Barbara.

'Why was that?' I asked, as this information was new to me.

'My parents were on their way to our christening and they met Martha, a village woman, outside the church. She stopped to look at us babies and she asked them what we were going to be called. My mother told her that we were going to be named Sally and Sarah; but Martha said that those names were very popular. She suggested that we should be called Beatrice and Barbara instead. My parents decided, there and then, that they preferred those names, so that was that,' said Barbara. 'We were baptised as Beatrice and Barbara.'

I couldn't help feeling a little dubious about this story. Then I thought about my great grandma Blanche with three young daughters already, Louisa, Frances and Mary. She would be preoccupied with the running of a small farm and taking her new-born twins to work at the hall, in a basket. She wouldn't have had much time to consider many names. Maybe it was true after all. A rare photo in my grandmother's album showed her as a tiny woman with a yoke on her shoulders, transporting pails of milk back from the farm.

It was at this moment that Robert and Julia's mother, Sally, rapped on the front door.

'Come forward,' called Barbara in her high pitched voice and charming Edwardian fashion.

There was a quaint, almost spooky, feeling to the old house.

'Don't go into the second attic,' Barbara would warn my cousin and me. The house had three floors and this room was on the top floor, at the far end, and unsafe. We'd also been told that my great grandfather had died in that room. We would tread cautiously up the staircase, reacting to every creaking floorboard or a shadow on the stairs, on the look-out for ghosts, and gingerly open the door to the attic. Barbara was right to warn us not to go in there, as the floor had caved in.

There were remnants of a bygone age everywhere. Warming pans were hanging on the walls, Victorian jugs and chamber pots in every room as the house had no bathroom; only an outside toilet in the front yard. There were mahogany dressing tables, some strewn with cobwebs and a faint musty scent hanging in the air.

My mother and I once went into the drawing room to fetch some soap from the bottom drawer of a cabinet. The tablets had been nibbled by mice but lying next to them, untouched, was Barbara's trousseau.

'I didn't know she was going to get married,' I whispered.

'She was courting a man called Willis for many years,' replied my mother. 'He used to visit her on Sundays as he lived in a different village. But their relationship fizzled out.'

I picked up the lacy embroidered garments and held them to my face, closing my eyes as I did so. A feeling of sadness came over me as I thought of Barbara's lost dreams, although she never spoke of them.

There was always a warm welcome from Barbara and offers of tea, lemonade, sweets, cakes and biscuits. As a child I would be offered white bread, spread with butter and sprinkled with white sugar. Barbara's personal favourite snack was bread dipped in dripping which would horrify today's health professionals; yet Barbara lived well into her eighties.

Barbara lived in a different age and never really kept up with the present. However, she shared my love of football and would sometimes borrow our television to watch a match. Our offer to buy her a television set was declined, as her life was full with her frequent visitors and the reading of the daily newspaper. It's easy to have a rosy view of the past, but it seemed that Barbara's early life symbolised an era of poverty, social inequality, servitude and strict social barriers. Yet there were good things too: a friendliness, neighbourliness and a sense of community.

I recall seeing the ambulance pull up outside her door and Barbara being taken away on a stretcher. She'd had a fatal stroke. She had outlived my grandmother by six years and for me in many ways, she was a surrogate. In the company of unmarried, childless Barbara I did not have to compete for attention with my six cousins, five of them being older than me. I felt that Barbara, in a sense, was mine.

Aunt Barbara wasn't particularly pretty or clever or talented in any way, yet she was popular because of her kindness, her generosity and her Edwardian quirkiness. In her parlour you almost felt you could go back in time and feel safe; protected by her compassionate company.

Over the years my memories of Aunt Barbara never dimmed, and she influenced my life more than she could ever know. Today I awoke at dawn and heard the birds chirping cheerfully outside my window. I thought of Aunt Barbara and I knew that all of that was in the past, whereas here I was welcoming in the future and a new morning. But I realized that, in my dreams at least, Great-Aunt Barbara would always be sitting in her parlour waiting for me to visit, and that I still have my wonderful memories of her.

MARY EASTEY
AND REBECCA NURSE

Lyn McKinney

Leaving town Plough Monday,
Sisters board the Rose of Yarmouth,
A stepping stone to loftier worlds.
A crescent moon hangs low
Over pitch black waters of the Yare,
Guiding their path to the stars.

Ropes cast, sails flap and salt spray flies,
The brig's away on the rising tide
And the lights of familiar places
Fall away in deepening gloom.
Families huddle below creaking decks
As the cradle rocks ominously.

Father Towne keeps a wakeful watch,
A mission book his faithful friend.
Was it God who called them to Salem?
His daughters dream in their rough woollen shawls,
Their pale, innocent arms entwined,
Oblivious to their dark destiny.

Six bells. A bleak, uncaring morning unfolds.
Only the brave are on deck to see it;
Rough seas break across the bow,
Making the timbers creak in pain.
There are few takers for the rye bread
And thin, grey slops of soup.

Six year old Mary holds Rebecca's hand,
Lest she should lose her frail footing
And be pulled overboard by sea serpents.
But her big sister keeps them at bay,
With stories of lions and tigers,
And kindly strangers in foreign lands.

For in that country of divine providence,
Father Towne will build his church
In a rough place by a cool river.
A community will spring from the reeds,
Tight, unforgiving and blind to the injustice
His daughters will suffer.

Fifty years on, await lies and deceit
And a thousand denials of intent.
Before death by the hangman's noose
Cuts short their principled lives,
After Salem's children point and scream,
And curse their elders for unnatural acts.

Will Rebecca remember her months at sea
As she mounts the wooden scaffold?
Will her sister fall on her lifeless face
And wonder why God should mock them thus,
By bringing them here, so far from home,
To better lives and early graves?

*This is based on fact – sisters Mary Eastey and Rebecca Nurse
(married names) left Great Yarmouth for the New World
around 1640, and were defendants in the Salem witch trials
in Massachusetts. Rebecca Towne Nurse was executed by
hanging in July 1692. Her younger sister Mary Towne Eastey
died the same way two months later.*

WE SHALL NOT GROW OLD

Mary Maynes

This was great. I was off on holiday with the boys, sailing on the wine dark sea. Fantastic. There were sixteen of us on the trip. More men than women and the imbalance seemed great to me. All I had to do was to be there and let them play as they wanted. No responsibility for me.

We were flying from Stansted, not too early. We got there in plenty of time so, after checking in, we went straight to Wetherspoons for breakfast. We raised our glasses.

'Nothing like the first breakfast beer.' And 'Cheers!' all round. We were on our way.

The first two nights we stayed in a hotel before we took charge of the yachts that we had hired for the week. It was great sitting by the pool, sipping our drinks and planning where we would sail. After a relaxing day we had arranged to eat on a long table by the pool, and the staff were busy setting it up for us. We began to sit down.

'Nigel, why don't you sit nearer the middle, then you will be able to hear the conversation better,' said Anne. He looked up startled, 'Don't you patronise me.'

He pushed his chair backwards and stormed off.

'What was all that about?' I asked.

'I don't know, but he's gone,' Anne replied.

'OK.' We continued to have a great, if not entirely sober, evening.

The next morning we didn't see Nigel, or George who was sharing his room. At lunch time George appeared.

'Where have you been? What have you been doing?'

'Playing nursemaid to Nigel. The police found him in the middle of the night, drunk in the road. He had his hotel key in his pocket, so they knew where to bring him.'

'What! How is he now?'

'He still seems drunk. I've been to the chemist to get some rehydrating salts.'

'Does he need a doctor?'

'He won't have one. He seems to be recovering now, but he appears to resent any help.' George had been having a difficult day coping with an ungrateful Nigel, when he could have been celebrating his birthday. He was seventy four.

The next day we went to the marina to collect the two boats. They were beautiful, with four double cabins on each. The two captains and their seconds-in-command checked the boats with the yacht company representatives, while we ladies went to the supermarket to get enough provisions to last for the week. The men insisted that we bought slabs of beer and lots of ice. We concentrated on breakfast and lunch food.

Sailing is so beautiful. So silent in a good breeze; we took it in turns to take the helm, while the men discussed navigation. I didn't care where I went, I just loved to watch the different colours of the rocks and foliage as we passed the islands, the changing shades and depth of the sea, sea birds, fish; and there was great excitement when we were occasionally accompanied by dolphins.

After a fabulous day, we arrived at our first destination. Mooring can be the hardest part of sailing, especially when we only get practice at doing it this way round once a year, when we are on holiday. After several approaches we moored successfully and were ready to sup Pimm's on deck, then prepare for an evening ashore. The two boats were moored next to each other, with the gang planks sloping down from the stern to the wobbly jetty.

We were ready to disembark. First problem – Michael couldn't walk down the gang plank on the other boat as his knees were giving him too much trouble. Of course he didn't say that, but simply said 'I don't think I'll come ashore this evening. I'll just find provisions to eat and drink on board.' We left him. After all, he's seventy and a grown up.

Nigel disembarked without difficulty, but George approached the narrow gangplank with a fixed smile on his face and it became apparent that his balance was so poor that it was pure luck that he didn't fall in. We walked around the bay en masse, and found an interesting, rustic restaurant that could accommodate fifteen people. No, sixteen, for now Michael had joined us.

'How did you get ashore?' we all wondered. He didn't say, but when we returned to our vessels he walked up a much wider gangplank on an adjacent vessel, then climbed over the gunnels onto his own boat. George observed this, and did the same, except he wobbled so much he looked as if he might fall between two of the boats.

The next morning Michael had perfected his technique, and took himself off for breakfast in a café. We ladies swam in the bay before preparing breakfast on board. As I lay on my back in the water looking up at the mountains I thought how beautiful the different shades of colour looked on the rocks. George didn't risk the gangplank. Chatting over breakfast, we realised that Nigel didn't know that he had missed a whole day of our holiday. He questioned why we had spent only one day at the hotel when we had planned two.

I liked to read on board, look out to sea, to sail, take the helm and chat. The other girlies preferred to be foredeck floozies, working on their tans. It was a holiday where we all did what we liked.

*

It is the following winter. The sailing group is together again, but today we are running. Well, some are running and some are walking through the woods. The route is a five mile circular trail, starting and ending at a pub. Michael used to run marathons, but can't do them anymore. He starts at the pub, walks for about ten minutes then goes back to the pub for a bottle of wine. George runs through the woods with his wobbly gait, but unfortunately trips over a tree root and returns covered in mud.

'No, I didn't trip. I just decided to get muddy.' Nigel is still running, though no longer at the front. I walk along, chatting to Brian. Suddenly we are accosted by someone who is possibly the landowner. We are on a public footpath, so this is strange.

'Oi! What are you doing? You can't walk here. Private land.'

'No, that's not the case. This is a public footpath.' The two men square up to each other, looking aggressive.

Oh no, what shall I do? I stand between the two men, and the young chap glares at me. I say, 'You wouldn't hit an old man.' He looks shamefaced and backs off. We continue on our walk. Brian is furious with me.

'What do you mean, calling me an old man?' remarks Brian. We stride through the woods in silence.

Another year passes. We sailed last year without Nigel, Michael, George and Brian. All gave good reasons. Nothing to do with ageing. Nigel had a stroke, and although he made a good recovery he lost his confidence, and couldn't make decisions. First he booked his place on board, then said no, then decided yes, by which time it was no longer available.

As we walk together through a field one day, he tells me that what he needs is to find a new partner. Then he would have a reason to get up in the morning. The trouble is he is so unrealistic. He has always prided himself on fitness and vigour. He was always a man for flirting, but now flirting doesn't have the desired effect, especially on the younger women whom he seems to think might be interested. He always thought that he was immortal. It is very difficult for him to accept that he is not. He is hankering after his youth and vitality, and is therefore anxious and depressed. He is fighting the inevitable. Do we all do that? It's easy to say, 'Enjoy this lovely day, this beautiful walk, your very good friends.' Much harder to achieve when you haven't got what you desire most.

I admire their spirit. 'We shall not grow old. We will walk, run, (when possible), sail, socialise, get drunk, live life to the full.' Should realism have to come into it? Should one make concessions to an ageing body? Should one change one's self image as time passes?

George is outraged. 'I had a letter today informing me of an appointment with the NHS Medicine for the Elderly department. Well, they can shove their appointment where the sun don't shine, because the very fact that they use such a designation betrays a total lack of understanding of the issues affecting people beyond the first flush of youth.' *Discuss.*

OVER THE HILL

Shirley Valentine Jones

'Over the hill,' they said.
'She's past it!'
'Nothing to say
Of interest.'
'Used to be OK'
'Like talking to a thick
 Brick wall.'
'Doesn't get the joke
 Anymore.'

Over the hill, for me,
Is fantastic.
Greener grass.
Greener everything.
Makes my seeing sing.
I see in super colour,
I notice small things
Magnified.

My hearing went early,
No one noticed –
Not even me.
Then I missed the pay off
Line of jokes.
I began to talk more –
To avoid listening.
But fewer people heard me –
They were on to the next thing –
Isolating.

Being on my own is relaxing
Listening drains energy.
Over the Hill
Is satisfyingly quiet.
Over the Hill?
But I'm climbing,
Still.

RUBY'S
REALLY RATHER AVERAGE DAY

Scott King

The view from Ruby's bungalow was spectacular in just how unspectacular it was. It was pretty bleak, truth be told. It overlooked the beach, which would have been fine if it wasn't for the derelict funfair that stood in front of it. The funfair had been disused and abandoned for many years and no one in the town knew why it hadn't just been taken away, it'd got to the point where residents had just forgotten about it. There was some kind of beautiful, yet depressing, irony about that. Ruby remembered the funfair as it was. Bright lights, noise from the overworked rides, and the joyful squeals from the children who enjoyed it. Her own children. It was tired looking now though. The vibrant colours had given way to faded paintwork and the green grass was now patchy and brown. Ruby smiled wistfully as it occurred to her that it mirrored her own life. Once rich, but now empty and full of sadness.

Ruby's husband had died six months ago due to complications during a heart bypass operation and now she was on her own; well save for Trixie, her beloved Yorkie. Mind you, Trixie was not getting any younger. If you'd asked Ruby if she thought she'd be living alone at seventy-two, having buried her husband and two children, she'd have thought you were crazy. Not that she thought seventy-two was young, just that she was so happy that she just wouldn't have been able to conceive of it. As she continued to stare out of the window, her thoughts turned to her children and how she and Ted used to take them to the fair, before they died. Their eyes would light up at the very suggestion of going to the fair and it was always the best time. It didn't even matter if it was raining, Ann and Rupert would embrace every little thing the fair had to offer. That was children for you, Ruby thought to herself as she picked up a photo from her window sill. The photo was of a young girl with red plaited hair and a boy with round glasses, both were smiling and young. It was the last photo Ruby had taken of them. They were twelve and fifteen when they died. Ann contracted leukaemia and Rupert was hit by a car.

Grief can do funny things to people. In some cases it unites them and sometimes it rips them apart. For Ted and Ruby, it did both. They split after Ann's passing but when Rupert died, their grief united them. They saw it as a silver lining but both joked in times of strife, 'You have to *really* want to see it'. After the children died, they were inseparable; they saw it as their duty. They were loved by their neighbours and Ruby's neighbours rallied round her on a daily basis. Sometimes to the point of suffocation.

'Right, old girl, that's enough reminiscing,' she exclaimed and got up from her chair by the window. She picked up her handbag and keys, and headed for the door. She got in her car and headed for the shops. She smiled at the locals as she helped herself to fresh fruit and veg, paid Vanessa, the shop girl, and left smiling ...

*

The red dilapidated car drove haphazardly down the road. The driver appeared, peering over the steering wheel. She was easily seventy years old and, on the basis of her limited vision over the windscreen, stood little higher than five foot two. She wore a cardigan she'd had for fifty years and her skin had the appropriate amount of wrinkles for a woman of her age. She had curly, grey hair tinted purple, large glasses and carried with her an unsettling aroma of lavender and marzipan. A string of cars started to line up behind her, the drivers of which were all trying, and failing, to second guess her erratic driving. She indicated that she was going to pull over and did so. She stopped and then emerged from the car. She wore a tunic dress with purple tights, matching shoes and a beige-coloured shawl. With the way fashions come back around and repeat themselves nowadays, she actually looked quite stylish. The drivers of the cars which had been behind her stopped at some lights and some yelled at her for her reckless driving. She smiled sweetly and apologised for holding them up. One woman asked if she was all right, as there was no obvious reason as to why she had pulled over. She ignored the question and reached into the car for something. She appeared once again, only now she was no longer smiling and was armed with a sawn off shotgun. She shot at the drivers who had taunted her, in the same haphazard way she had driven. The once quiet suburban street, which was two minutes ago covered in shades of autumn, was now a threatening shade of crimson red.

*

No one will ever know what made Ruby snap that day because after gunning down six people, she turned the gun on herself. That was Ruby's anything but really rather average day.

HOMECOMING

Rupert Mallin

I'm someone
Who would never miss
My own homecoming
Arriving home
I read all the greetings
Awaiting me

At bed time
Having been away
I set and kiss my bedside clock

Goodnight
And then turn her face
Knowing that she
Will provide me
Morning tea in bed

I'm someone
Who enjoys the mornings
Especially when I've been away
Kindly, the landing light
Has been left on for me
To negotiate the bathroom, dressing
And other preparations for the day
And this is a special day
Because I'm going away

I'm someone
Who prepares for going away
And have left instructive post-it notes
For they say
I may return home
One day soon

JOSEPHINE

Lyn Hazleton

The dressmaking scissors lay open on the kitchen work-surface. Veronica put them there before leaving for work. When she returned home later that day, they would be the first thing she'd pick up.

Despite the unwelcome intrusion of the scissors being placed next to her, Josephine continued to eat her breakfast, purring deeply, her tail swishing side to side. Apart from the very tip of her tail which was china-white, Josephine's fur was blue-black. *Witch-Cat Josie,* Charles often called her whenever something unexplained happened in the house. It was his wont to tease and Veronica, who liked to appease, would oblige by scooping Josephine up in her arms and threading her around her neck in mock horror. It was a silly ritual, one they'd begun nineteen years ago when they'd first brought Josephine home as a kitten.

When she'd finished her breakfast and cleaned her whiskers, Josephine stretched and arched her spine high. Giving the scissors a swipe with her paw, setting them spinning, she turned and, with her tail held erect, tiptoed a path around the toaster, the teapot and the used mugs. At the edge of the sink, she paused momentarily before leaping over the washing-up bowl and landing daintily on the draining board where she proceeded to lap up the milk in Veronica's cereal bowl. After she finished, she dropped down the side of the work surface onto the floor, padded past the French windows and onto her bed where she curled around herself and settled down to sleep. The tip of her tail flicked to and fro, like a wagging finger, then slowed and tucked itself between her front paws. All became quiet and still while Josephine slept the day away.

Meanwhile, at the office, Veronica was running through her plan. When her sister told her about Charles and his sordid affair, it was as if a spike had been driven into her side. Tears dropped into her upturned hands as she sat with the telephone in her lap. Margaret was very sorry to be the one to give her the news, but Charles's indiscretions at the golf club were becoming more than a risky blunder of casual flirtation. She felt it her duty to let Veronica know before people started talking behind her back and, besides, wasn't it better to find out from family? Veronica wasn't sure, but as her tears dried, her rage grew. He'd humiliated her; the girl was barely more than a teenager, as Margaret so readily pointed out. Veronica chose to bide her time and carried on as if nothing was amiss; keeping house and cooking dinner.

In the weeks since receiving Margaret's phone call, Veronica considered all her options before making a decision and now everything was mapped out. She was pleased she'd waited; she knew for certain what would upset Charles the most and today she was ready to act out her revenge. Veronica's only concern was for Josephine but, she reminded herself, it was best for Josephine to stay with Charles where things were familiar.

Veronica picked up the phone and made the call to her sister to remind her she'd be arriving later that evening to stay as arranged. Then she left the office. With knuckles of white stone on the steering wheel she drove home, oblivious to the rush hour traffic as she visualised her next movements.

Veronica dropped her bag in the hallway and went into the kitchen where Josephine was sitting next to the scissors, meowing her welcome. Veronica went over to fuss her and after several long strokes from the top of her head, she allowed her fingers to curl loosely around Josephine's tail, feeling it run through her hand. Josephine purred, pushing her body against Veronica's arm.

'No, no more Josephine,' Veronica said as she nudged her away and picked up the scissors. Bringing them up in front of her face, her chest tightened and her heart quickened. She flexed her fingers watching as the scissor blades slid together smoothly and sweetly. She repeated the motion several more times until holding the scissors felt natural and easy. She was ready.

In the bedroom she stood in front of the mirrored doors with Josephine warm against her leg. She looked into her own eyes; they were green flecked with gold – *Josephine's eyes,* Charles teased her many times. She pursed her lips together in a tight pucker. Despite her poise and determination, she could feel no spark for what she was about to do. The light in her had been extinguished.

Shaking Josephine loose from her ankle, she stepped forward and opened Charles's wardrobe. At once she was enveloped by his smell; a concoction of cigarettes, pine cologne and spent alcohol. Clenching and opening her fist, the scissor blades sliced together. As Veronica's resolve grew, her hesitation fell away. She would do this thing. She would do it now.

Charles's jackets hung like her silent witnesses. Veronica was insulted by their defiance: an array of fabrics; tweed, corduroy, satin and velvet in a rainbow of navy-blue, scarlet, green and purple. A cacophony of styles; double breasted, single breasted, long line and wide lapel – Charles's passion, his collection acquired over many years, lovingly sourced from antique markets and auctions. She'd humoured him all these years, pretended she didn't know it wasn't just an act of vanity. Like a peacock fanning out its feathers as part of a courtship ritual, Charles was attracting mates. But no more, no longer would she be humiliated, no longer would she live in their sham of a marriage.

Cutting off the sleeves was simple, a rhythmic task that soothed Veronica as she worked her way along the rails, taking each sleeve in turn. Snip. Snip. She was rigorous and precise with her cutting, like a dressmaker preparing fabric. She didn't rush, rather she savoured her time spent with each jacket, with every cut and slice of the blades. There was no hurry. The floor of Charles's wardrobe soon became a carpet of colour and texture as each sleeve fell to its resting place. At the last jacket, she paused. It was purple velvet, sumptuous and beguiling. Releasing her grip, she put the scissors down, took up handfuls of material in her fists and buried her face into the soft folds. On the floor of the wardrobe Josephine frolicked amongst the fabric cuttings, stalking imaginary mice, her tail swishing back and forth.

Veronica couldn't bring herself to say goodbye to Josephine. She picked up her case and left. Later when she arrived at Margaret's house, she started to shake. It began at her fingers. They trembled as she took a cigarette out of the packet and put it to her lips. The flame from her lighter wavered alarmingly. The trembling turned into shaking and became violent spasms. Margaret helped her into bed, gave her a hot water bottle, staying with her until finally she slept.

The next morning, Veronica sat by the window looking out onto Margaret's garden. The leaves were falling. Winter was on the horizon. She noticed the birds on the feeder and thought about Josephine. She flicked over the pages of her magazine without seeing, occasionally wetting her index finger against the inside of her bottom lip. An ashtray on the table by her side overflowed with half smoked cigarettes. The tea in the teapot was cold.

'This was on the door step.' Margaret walked into the room and put a parcel on the table. She placed her hand on Veronica's arm and squeezed. 'There's no point in brooding Veronica, what's done, is done. I expect this is from Charles. Do you want me to stay with you while you open it?' She patted Veronica on the shoulder and followed her gaze through the window and to the bird feeder.

'Look at the robin, Margaret. Isn't he lovely?'

'Veronica. Didn't you hear me?'

'No. What?'

'You have a parcel. From Charles. Open it. I'll be in the kitchen if you need me.'

'Margaret, do you think …' Veronica's voice trailed away as she heard Margaret close the door, leaving the fragrance of rosewater hanging in the air.

Veronica left her cigarette burning in the ashtray and picked up the parcel, instantly recognising Charles's handwriting, one word – *Veronica*. She held the parcel in her hand, gauging its weight. It was heavy. She assessed its shape; there was something long and hard inside. She frowned. Her heart began to quicken. She felt moist in her arm pits. She slid a finger nail under the lip of the fold and teased the parcel open. She reached inside and pulled out her dressmaking scissors, but there was something else in there, at the bottom. She shook the parcel and a small packet wrapped in tissue paper fell into her lap. She picked it up. Her heart was hammering now, beating from within the confines of her chest like a bird. Veronica understood even before she unwrapped it. Fear rained down on her like a shower of arrows. She held the white bloodied end of Josephine's tail between her fingers, brought it to her cheek and howled.

THE MOUNTAIN OF LIFE

Gill Wilson

out of the darkness
I take a breath; eyes open
and my life begins

The lights are too bright. I cry. I feel unsettled, uncomfortable and hungry. My arms and legs feel disconnected from me. I am confused. I sleep. Watching and imitating, I open my mouth and sounds emerge: I gurgle, I laugh, I form words. My legs wobble. I tire quickly and fall but I persist and get stronger. Everything is new and interesting, full of wonder. I grow and learn and get wiser. I study, have opinions, become independent and find my direction: I am me. At work and home I am fulfilled. I have a circle, within a circle, of carefully chosen people.

here at the summit
the pinnacle of my life;
spectacular views

The family grows and becomes more disparate. My offspring explore their potential and make their own circles within circles. The workplace is busier. New employees, young and keen, crammed with technological know-how. I am yesterday's star. Words escape me. My legs wobble. I tire quickly and fall. I persist but get weaker. My memory ails. Goals are changed; achievements diminished. The circle within my circle has evaporated. The lights are too bright. I feel unsettled. I am uncomfortable and hungry. My arms and legs feel disconnected from me. I am confused. I sleep.

into the darkness
my breathing ceases; eyes close
and my life ends

OLD DOG

Phil McSweeney

A sheepdog cross of some kind, she'd been forced to retire early with him. She'd exchanged the free run of the countryside for a clipped afternoon stroll round the park alongside his mobility scooter; and an hour sitting by his bench. She used to have a name but that had been retired too. Old Dog was good enough. The old dog had seen almost everything of the last fifteen years. A frisky rescue pup for Nathaniel's older son's fifth birthday, she'd lived every moment of the boys' childhoods. She'd retrieved their sticks and punctured their footballs. She'd showered them in mud and licked their faces clean. She'd swum with them in forbidden rivers and kept her silence. Dumped for new girlfriends, she'd taken them back every time. Coming to work daily with him for twelve years, she'd been Nathaniel's faithful companion until he couldn't work any longer. These mornings she patiently waited for him to dress, follow his routine, and get his breath back - until they managed the park in the afternoon. Now, weathered together, they watched the whistling wind herd the soulless leaves at its will.

THE FIELD

Lyn McKinney

The back gate is swinging wide open on its hinges. Dolls lie abandoned on the grass, their soulless faces gazing up at the sky, mini tea cups and plates strewn across the path. I'm staring at an empty back garden in disbelief. Where is Orla? I left my daughter happily playing with her toys. For a moment I think I'm dreaming. Then reality kicks in. Maybe she got distracted by something in the field opposite. I screw up my eyes in an effort to see across the lane into the meadow, my hand shutting out the sun which is beating down.

She must be playing games. Six-year-olds love hide and seek – that's it. She's crouched down behind some large mound of grass, her tanned face full of expectancy, waiting for me to find her. A light breeze is blowing across the field, gently bending the tips of the meadow flowers and grasses. Surely she hasn't gone far.

'Well,' I say loudly, crossing the lane, and then the ditch into the field, trying to avoid the nettles, 'I wonder where Orla is ... it's almost tea time and Daddy will be home soon with fish and chips.' A ploy usually guaranteed to provoke a reaction. Nothing.

I'm shouting now. 'Orla! Come on please darling, it's getting late.' I stumble to the top of the field to get a better view of the surrounding land. No sound except for the chaffinches pink-pinking in the warm afterglow of a midsummer day. No sign of her.

Now I'm worried. She's not a child to run off – she likes to know that someone's there, keeping an eye on her, and we've told her time and time again the importance of not going off with strangers. Maybe she's returned to the house and she's slumped in front of the TV, waiting for me to make tea. I race back, my heart thumping, barely concealed panic rising inside.

My neighbour Mary is walking down to meet me. 'Helen,' she says 'Have you seen Sam?' I shake my head. Sam is a playmate of Orla's. They're often found in one another's gardens, playing games, racing round together. 'He was with me in the kitchen one minute, and gone the next,' says Mary, 'I've searched everywhere. Why would he just run off like that?' She's close to tears.

'Mary, I can't find Orla either.' We stare at each other for a minute, hoping they might be together.

We begin a frantic search of both houses, turning them upside down, our hearts racing, willing the children to be hiding under a bed or in a wardrobe, ready to leap out on us and shout, 'Surprise!' But it's eerily quiet.

Mary's partner Jim goes round to close neighbours, asking them to check their properties. I call Matt. He's not picking up. He must be on his way home. I leave a voicemail. 'Matt, Orla's gone missing.' Just saying the words out loud is starting to make it horribly real. He gets back to me within two minutes. 'I'm at the chippie,' he says. 'What's happened?'

The car wheels scrunch on the gravel as he scorches into the close ten minutes later. He and Jim cover every inch of the field, shouting the children's names until I can't bear to listen anymore. I call friends, parents of Orla's school friends, aunts and uncles, Orla's head teacher. It's now an hour since they vanished.

Mary is distraught, blaming herself for not keeping a sharp enough eye on Sam, saying it's her punishment for having had an abortion two years previously. Normally a personal confession like that would lead to some kind of supportive neighbourly chat, but not today. I'm not in the mood for soul-baring and guilt trips. 'No, of course, it's not punishment Mary,' I snap. 'You're just worried about Sam.' And then I feel bad and make tea, trying to ignore the dread that's mounting inside. Horrible images are flashing through my mind – suppose they've been kidnapped, or enticed away by some paedophile? My chest feels like it's having to pull a heavy load, and I feel sick.

Matt and Jim return. I can tell from their exhausted, downcast faces, their search has been fruitless. 'OK,' says Matt, 'it's time to call the police.'

Within a few minutes two policewomen are with us wanting information and recent photographs. I find one of Orla taken at her last birthday party. As I hand it over, the nightmare is starting to sink in. It's not some awful dream. Our little girl really has disappeared. Her heart-breaking smile is seared across my brain and her curly brown hair and freckled nose shine out of the frame, reducing me to a crumpled heap.

A policewoman radios for back-up and sniffer dogs, before they begin a painstaking search of both houses and gardens, neighbouring sheds and garages, as well as the field opposite. As the light begins to fade there is an army of people assisting them. The lane is full of police cars, lights flashing, officers using crackling talkback.

At around nine o'clock, one of the policewomen comes to our door. There's no news, but then she says, 'It's an odd one, this. It seems your children aren't the only ones missing. We've had calls from another four families saying the same thing. We've got half the county police out looking for them. And they all disappeared around the same time. Can you think of *anywhere* they might have gone? Friends? A relative? Grandparents?'

Grandparents! I have to let Mum know before anyone else does. I pick up my mobile. 'Mum?' She sounds tired. I open my mouth, not trusting myself to speak immediately. Trying to keep a steady voice, I go over the events of the afternoon with her. There's silence at the other end. She's devastated, I can tell. She wants to be with us, and feels so much further away than the other side of town. Promising to keep in touch, I put down the phone, saying I'll call her later.

Matt has been out searching for hours. He arrives back, tired and alone. As the light fades slowly to black, I'm starting to shake, thinking of Orla out there, without a coat, cold and scared. She doesn't like the dark. We have to keep a light on at night. Through the living room windows, I can see squad cars lined up outside, their radios blaring. They're talking about dragging the river, a mile away. When I hear that, my blood runs cold. Matt, normally my rock, sits white-faced and motionless in an arm chair, an empty whisky glass beside him. 'You know, you hear these awful cases where young children go missing, but you never think it's going to happen to you. Where's our baby, Helen?' And the tears trickle down his face.

We have to stay positive. It's my survival mechanism. 'Matty look, we don't know anything. Lots of children are missing, so the chances are that they're safe somewhere.' I try and keep my voice calm – Jesus, who am I trying to convince? As I speak, I can see searchlights sweeping the end of the field, on the brow of the hill.

The phone rings and we both leap up. It's my mother. 'No Mum, nothing.' In spite of everything, we both fall into an uneasy doze in the early hours – me on the sofa, Matt in his chair.

I wake with a jolt. Someone is touching my arm, stroking it softly and singing. It's Orla's voice, the one she uses when she sings to her teddy bear. I can sense the early brightness of a rising sun, and there is a smell of bonfire in the room. Opening my eyes slowly I see my daughter, fully clothed, sitting on the floor beside me, one arm laid gently on mine without a care in the world. 'Orla,' I whisper, 'is that you?' She smiles and I spring up from my seat, gather her in my arms and hug her fiercely.

'Mummy stop, stop, I can't breathe.' By now Matt is awake and we're both crying with relief. We sit as a trio on the lounge floor and hug and laugh and hug again. Orla seems amused but unfazed. 'I'm hungry Mummy. Can I have some Rice Krispies?'

Matt goes to see the police outside. None of them can work out how Orla slipped into the house without being seen. As she sits swinging her legs and eating her cereal, I ask her where she's been. She smiles. 'Playing – with the other children. Is there any toast?'

'Which children? Sam?' I try and keep it casual. Don't want to frighten her.

'Yes, and some others. They had funny clothes. But we did lots of singing and dancing in the field. Didn't you see us?'

'No darling, I didn't. Who were the children in funny clothes?'

'I don't know. But they were friendly. We had lots of fun.'

'Where did you go when it got dark?'

'Oh we went back to their house and had tea. Not as nice as ours,' she added, biting into her toast and honey.

Later in the day the police tell us the other missing children are also back at home. All of them talk of playing with children in strange clothes, but none of them can say where they've been. It's a mystery. I make Orla promise never to leave the back garden again without me.

A few months later, I'm in the local post office with Mr Goodman, who's been village postmaster for decades. 'Oh yes,' he says, 'our son James and his wife joined the search team that night. None of us liked to think of young children out all night. Such a worry for you all. And you say she just turned up the next morning?'

I'm nodding. 'Anyway they're home, safe and sound. It was a frightening experience for us all, though.'

As I speak, I catch a whiff of smoke from someone's pipe outside the post office. It reminds me of the smell in the air when Orla woke me that morning. 'That's funny,' I muse, 'I'd forgotten that. There was a definite smell of bonfire when Orla returned. It soon disappeared though.'

Mr Goodman goes quiet. 'The children said they'd been playing with other children in funny clothes? And it was Midsummer Day?'

'What is it Mr Goodman? Do you know something?' He's clearly hesitant to say any more but I urge him to go on.

'Well, way back in Victorian times, there was a family living at the farm which owned the field opposite you. Quite a large family. One night one of the farmhands, who lodged with them, left a lantern too near a bale of hay in one of the outhouses and the whole lot went up, the house and all. The farmer and his wife survived but they lost six children in the fire, all under the age of ten. It was midsummer, with very little water about and the place burned down in minutes. Poor mites, they never stood a chance.'

'How do you know all this?'

'It was Mrs Goodman's great grandfather had the farm. Her grandfather was born after the fire. He was an only child, but we always knew there'd been brothers and sisters.'

The next day I'm in the library. Surely a fire like that would have made the papers? The library assistant smiles encouragingly. 'The fire at Butlers' farm? Yes, that was June 1897. It made the front page of the local paper and the nationals. Desperately sad.' She finds the paper for me. I take it over to the light to see more clearly. The headline reads 'Six Children Lost in Farm Fire.' And there's a black and white photograph. Sitting cross-legged in Victorian clothes in front of Mr and Mrs Butler, in the back garden of the farmhouse, are Orla, Sam and their friends.

MIXTAPE
A Radio Play

Scott King

Characters: Presenter
                      Jeremiah Flynn
                      Producer
                      Jeremiah's Manager

Studio 2, Radio Surf's Up. Truro, Cornwall.

Rehearsal: Tuesday October 16th, 2018, 10.00-17.30
Recording: Saturday October 20th, 2018, 10.00-16.00
Transmission: Saturday November 3rd, 2018, 13.00-14.00

Truro, Cornwall. A small, dingy recording studio.

A slightly dishevelled man in his early 40s shuffles in his seat while a younger, more trendy man arranges papers. Both are wearing headphones. Two other men are also present. An inoffensive jingle plays.

PRESENTER: Today on the Mixtape we have up-and-coming writer, Jeremiah Flynn. Welcome to the show, Jeremiah, thank you for being here.

JEREMIAH: (mumbles) Happy to be here.

Jeremiah's manager gives him a hard stare.

PRESENTER: Music touches everyone's lives and our listeners love to hear from their favourite authors, artists and musicians about their own experiences. Before the show, you were asked to think about a selection of songs that are important to you and the story behind them, so let's start the ball rolling. How did you find the process?

JEREMIAH: Difficult, to be honest with you. It's not that I'm dead inside, or that I don't have particular favourites. It's just that when I was asked to think of a story to go with them, I got a bit stuck.

PRESENTER: Oh, well I'm glad we invited you on the show!

JEREMIAH: My first song actually owes much to Desert Island Discs, where you clearly stole the idea for this feature from,

and its longest serving presenter, Sue Lawley. It's 'So
Lonely' by The Police. When I was younger I used to
think the refrain featured in that song was repeating the
name of the thinking man's crumpet of the late 80s,
Sue Lawley. It never occurred to me to question why
Gordon Sumner and his pals had written an ode to her
and when I realised the lyric was in fact, 'so lonely',
I was a little relieved.

PRESENTER: Thank you, Jeremiah. I'm sure Sue Lawley will be
               thrilled to hear that she was such an inspiration to
               you, but nowhere near as thrilled as my producer, who
               is off licking his wounds at you throwing shade at this
               feature.

The producer looks away.

JEREMIAH: What is 'throwing shade'?

Jeremiah's manager grimaces. Irritated.

PRESENTER: Throwing ...

JEREMIAH: Never mind, let's carry on. My second song is Eiffel 65's
               one and only hit, 'Blue (Da Ba Dee)'. The story here
               isn't very interesting I'm afraid, it just reminds me of
               being at University in Newcastle upon Tyne. I love
               Newcastle, I still visit regularly, and am still great friends
               with one or two of my old uni friends.

PRESENTER: Always nice to hold on to some memories, while you
               still can. I've never been to Newcastle myself.

JEREMIAH: (Winking) Maybe your mum will take you one day!
               My third song is actually a song I hate and it's 'Killing
               In the Name' by Rage Against The Machine. 'Killing
               In the Name' reminds me of an old haunt I used to
               frequent from the age of about 17 to 27, The Spiral.
               The Spiral was not a venue, it was a particular night
               held at a venue, and the music played was deemed to

be 'alternative'. Although I'm pretty sure the DJ did play Daphne and Celeste's 'Ooh Stick You' once. That went down well!

PRESENTER: (Smiling) There's no accounting for taste!

JEREMIAH: Quite! The 90s is the decade that music was most important to me, and my favourite band was the Irish rock band, The Cranberries. If you don't know The Cranberries, please don't be put off by the use of the word 'Irish', they were nothing like either U2 or The Corrs. Anyway, two of my friends and I had tickets to see The Cranberries (circa 1994) and, as it would have been the first concert we'd ever been to, we were pretty excited. However, at the last minute, the concert was cancelled because the singer, Dolores, had broken her leg. Anyway, about ten years on and The Cranberries were on hand to fuck with me again.

PRESENTER: I'd like to apologise for Jeremiah's language there, listeners.

JEREMIAH: What? Oh shit, yeah sorry. Where was I? Oh yeah, The Cranberries. They were due to play my student union but cancelled because Dolores had flu. More like bone idleness if you ask me. I suppose I'd been harbouring some resentment towards The Cranberries, especially Dolores, which was fine when she was alive but then she died and it became more difficult to be angry at her. Song four on my list is 'Zombie' by The Cranberries.

PRESENTER: Thank you again for that rather colourful tale, Jeremiah. Sadly, we are running out of time here on Radio Surf's Up.

JEREMIAH: You asked me to pick five songs, so I did.

PRESENTER: I'm sorry, I really don't think we ...

JEREMIAH: My last song is 'Life is a Rollercoaster' by Ronan
              Keating. My friends and I went to The Big Breakfast
              Roadshow in Great Yarmouth and Ronan was
              performing. We were keen to meet him so when he did
              a little walkabout of the park, I donned a bandana and
              pretended to be terminally ill in order to make that
              happen. I didn't actually say I was terminally ill, but
              with my bandana, pasty skin, and forlorn expression,
              it was kind of implied. Anyway, he took pity on us, well,
              me, and the mission was complete. Ronan Keating.
              What a guy!

*The producer flaps his hands wildly. Jeremiah's manager looks aghast and
makes an apologetic face towards the producer.*

PRESENTER: Er, thanks for joining us, Jeremiah. Jeremiah's collection
              of short stories is out now at all good book shops.

Jingle plays. Both men remove their headphones.

JEREMIAH: Am I going to be on one of those TV shows where
              presenters talk about their worst guests?

PRESENTER: Do you think you'll ever be famous enough to be
              referred to?

JEREMIAH: Nice shot. Cutting.

Jeremiah and his manager leave and the presenter looks at the producer,
who takes out a bottle of scotch and two tumblers.

MAGDALEN CEMETERY

Hilary Hanbury

Few flowers bloom in vases here.
Framed by red brick arches,
The dark grass beckons.
Memorials lean drunkenly,
Proclaiming the passing of a soul
And shrink as the century moves on.

Major Cockaday MC
Royal Artillery
And his son of 21
Who died of wounds at Cambrai in 1918
Reunited with Edith
At last, in 1958

A wounded angel rests against a cross
Sacred to the memory of a dear wife
'A tender Mother sleepest here'
Where faded words recede
Till only birth and death
Denote existence.

Yet still the sun lights every one.
The grey stone pillars every morning, warm.
As glinting shards, they welcome
Those who come after,
To lay their offerings
In silent grace and apology.

RESIDENTIAL CARE

Sophie Yeomans

I arrive to find you sitting
in a light and airy room;
your oak chair by the window
looking at the pond
guarded by a plastic heron.

Pink clematis climbs
into the sycamore,
and blossom from the cherry tree
settles softly in the grass.

You are content
to sit and let time drift by,
watching events roll past
as if on a distant screen.

I feel intrusive, distracting,
dragging contentment out of you;
engaging you in conversation,
when you prefer to dwell in quiet.

Then I realise it is not me
that you resist,
but the clamour of my anxiety
to get it right.

LOVE AFFAIR WITH TROUSERS

Shirley Valentine Jones

My love affair with trousers began at a very early age – I think I must have been only about three years old. This was 1937 and we were living in Chiswick at the time. My mother had taken my sister and me to visit a friend of hers who had a toddler son. I don't remember his name and I don't remember playing with him. We were probably only there because my mother and her friend needed some adult gossip and laughter after being trapped in their respective houses, caring for their small but hugely demanding children. I really don't remember anything about that visit except this:

The boy had short trousers on with a little narrow pocket of material poking out at the front. I wondered why it was there. Then, in a room which I recall as huge and sparsely furnished except for a potty in the corner by an easy chair in which his mother was sitting, the answer to the riddle confronted me. The infant boy had his trousers pulled down by his mother. She did it very skillfully while still laughing and talking with my mother. No warning, no fuss, no thought of privacy. The boy was fairly roughly seated on the potty – but not quite correctly. A little bit skew-whiff, a little bit off centre. Suddenly a spout of water went across the room. A strong arc and it came from an intriguing part of his body the boy had 'down below' which looked a bit like a little finger.

I was transfixed. I was curious. How wonderful, I thought, I can't do that. Now I knew what that little pocket of material was for – to keep that little extra bit of body snug and warm. That fountain of water is still in my memory today – sharp and clear. And the short cotton trousers with their extra flap at the front. For years I suspected it to be a false memory. But I now know, through recent internet research, that this did exist and was called a 'wee hole' or a 'penis pocket'.

The circus came to Chiswick when I was five years old. It was a full blown Romanian circus with animals, acrobats, clowns and pretty girls. My father booked tickets for all of us to go. The seats were banked and hard but we were near the front and my sister and I wore our pleated kilts – so they bunched up a bit and made the seat more comfortable. We saw elephants being utterly obedient, a lion in a cage with its keeper playing with it without seeming to feel any fear. We saw acrobats, way above our heads with sparkly outfits – both the men and the women – doing death-defying trapeze and tight-rope walking acts. But what I remember most of all are the clowns.

Their faces were rather frightening – especially when one of them clambered over the barrier – almost to our very seats and spoke to my sister (who was three years older than me). He made a joke, and everyone but us laughed. He was leaning right over me. His baggy pants were made of all sorts of coloured materials – squares and rounds and triangles of sparkling brightness. They had glistening jewels sewn on to them at random intervals so there was a diamond gleam about them. They flapped around his legs and smelled of sawdust and mustiness and animals. To me it was a magical smell and the trousers were brilliant in every way, and I wished I could have a pair like them. Later, when we got home, there was talk about the circus and in the middle of it I found myself asking my mother if I could have a pair of trousers like the clown. 'Don't be silly,' she said, 'girls don't wear trousers.' The song *Baggy Trousers* by Madness always reminds me of this clown.

Trousers became very important in my life when playing with the local boys in Selborne where my father was stationed during the war. I was eight years old; the year: 1942. In the school holidays my sister and I played with the local children, especially a small gang of friendly boys. They used to chase us, tease us, and then escape by running away – always faster than us. We just could not keep up. There were great clumps of stinging nettles where we used to play. Now we knew a lot about stinging nettles because our frugal mother used to pick the very tops of the young nettles and cook them like spinach to have with our dinner. To us they were horrible – very strong to taste – but very good for us, we were told. I think, judging by my sister's and my good health for nearly all our lives, my mother was right. They *were* very good for us. And we knew they stung – not when they had been boiled, but when fresh and growing in the fields. We helped to pick them and sometimes the sting went right through our woollen gloves. The boys always wore short trousers and I thought it would be great if my sister and I could run away from them – into the nettles – where they could not get to us. We asked our mother, who was a good seamstress, if she could make us some trousers. We explained why. By this time, women in trousers were common place because of the war, so she said she would.

Next time we played with the boys, we were armed in our nice cotton trousers – a sort of khaki colour – and right down to our ankles. This time when they pestered us and teased us, we had a haven to run to. We ran straight into the nettle beds. Not a sting did we feel. The boys dared not follow us. It felt like a victory. How I felt liberated in those trousers. They enabled me to feel equal to the boys. In fact, superior. Able to do what they could not do – and able to safely tease them.

I was always intrigued by the cowboys' outfits we saw in Western films. John Wayne was a big star then. He wore denims and, on top of them, leather 'chaps' which were like fishermen's waders but with a belt to join them together at the top. They covered the legs of the cowboy to protect him from chafing when riding for hours on his horse. But they left the front and back top part of the denim trousers uncovered and strangely emphasised the contours of the cowboy's bottom and crotch. As a teenager I thought they were a bit rude, but very attractive.

The American soldiers and airmen were in evidence towards the end of the war. Their uniforms were of a far superior cut than those of our British troops. They stood out as more slickly dressed – and they knew it. I was too young to ever get to know an American soldier or airman – I was only ten when the war finished – but I saw them from afar and liked what I saw;

particularly the sharp creases down the front of their trousers.

When I was twenty-one years old, I emigrated to Canada and I found life there much less formal than in England. In Calgary, we used to go out for breakfast rides. We could wear whatever we wanted – no jodhpurs here!

I then went on to emigrate to USA because I got a job on a newspaper in Kodiak Island, and for the first time, trousers became everyday wear – for work and for leisure. I lived with an American and his English wife and they introduced me to prospecting. George had the rights to several prospective tungsten mines and so, at weekends, we used to climb up the mountains wearing intriguing combat-like trousers with pockets for compasses and bottles of water and collected samples.

Now I am old, I am thinking of designing my own trousers. They would have a lot of pockets – like my Alaskan ones – but they would be made of wool, of a practical colour – definitely not purple. Perhaps, though, they would be baggy-comfortable and have a few sequins spotted around in memory of my clown. There would be a pocket for my keys, a small one for my credit card and cash, one for my handkerchief, pain killers and water – but two important additional pockets. Right over where my knees are there would be medium size pockets for mini hot water bottles. My knees need to be kept warm now. I wonder if there could a niche market for these trousers?

Hiding Places

Rupert Mallin

The Roman quarry at Hangman's Hill
An abandoned bakery, Chiltern
A small railway shed, Ashen
Behind the knoll, Mill Meadows
Everywhere in Hollow Ditch
On the landing behind the tallboy
Under others, backseat of the school bus
Beneath a tarpaulin in the factory yard
In a pub, the other side of Birdbrook
In an infection I invented one morning
In poetry and paint
On this ward
In your eyes
In these old bones

And found

On the back step with a beetroot sandwich
Camouflaged with coal dust in the coal shed
Throwing stubble bombs in Mr Lee's Field
Applying Chinese burns to Georgie's arm
In Doctor Reid's black lapboard waiting room
Hitch hiking during a school Civil Society class
Sick on bourbon on a bench in the cemetery
Rolling fags from my father's tin
Asleep under a tarpaulin in the factory yard
At the county court, swearing on a bible
Covered in poetry and paint
Alone on this ward
In this failing frame
In your sparkling eyes

Cynthia
Alone In Her Dining Room

Lyn Hazleton

Cynthia opens the door to her dining room and steps across the threshold. She shivers despite the room being bathed in autumn sunshine. Golden fingers of light strike the mahogany sideboard and point towards Cynthia's sewing desk where, in a wide shallow drawer along with her cotton reels and dressmaking pins, she keeps her tarot cards. They're safe in this drawer.

In Cynthia's hand is a duster, stiff and blackened. She knows she should change it, but judges it will last another day. She walks to the sideboard, opens a drawer and takes out a tin of polish. She loosens the lid with her fingernails, wipes wax on the duster and spreads it on the sideboard, working to a tune in her head. Whispered words escape unnoticed from her lip-sticked mouth and the room fills with a lavender loveliness. Her body sways as she polishes. She picks up an old black and white photograph in a silver frame of Gerald and Miriam when they were young. She brings the frame to her lips before replacing it with care. She turns and moves to the dining room table, stares past its glossy surface into its icy depths and meets her reflection. Her face is pale, cheek bones rouged in peach. Her indigo eyes are rimmed with kohl and her silver-streaked, dark brown hair is pulled back and fixed in a cruel way at the nape of her neck. Stray fly-away hairs float about her face. She erases the image with her duster and begins caressing the mirrored mahogany, tracing imagined circles, like those on the surface of a pebble-disturbed pond. A pulse beats at her temple and her breath quickens as she works the wax, rubbing with a strength that belies her thin frame. The amber beads around her neck knock against her chest. When she is satisfied the table is ready, she stands upright, puts her hands to her hips and arches her back. She looks about her. The only dust she can see is floating in the sunlight and she thinks this beautiful.

Sitting down to catch her breath, she rests her hands on the table, finger nails tapping. As she waits for her heart to steady, her mind wanders to a day earlier in the year when she and Miriam walked along a sea wall some-where in north Essex. It was late spring, a chilly day with a biting wind. There was a smell of rotting seaweed in the air. Miriam stopped abruptly, stepped in front of Cynthia, put her hands in the pockets of her red coat and said, 'Maybe you and Gerald should have had children.'

Cynthia replied straight away, 'Oh, don't be silly, Sweet. Gerald would have been a lousy father and besides there would have been no us.' Realising she'd said it out loud, here in her dining room, Cynthia glances over her shoulder, but Gerald isn't there. She wants to call out 'Miriam' but her throat tightens. She puts her fingers there. Tears threaten to spill, but she doesn't have time for this, not now; she needs to steady herself, to prepare.

Cynthia checks her watch. In another half an hour, the doorbell will ring. She imagines Miriam on the train from London, putting her book away, readying herself to get off at the next station. She thinks about Gerald, in the reading room of the library, glasses perched on the tip of his nose, buried deep in the research for his latest book, a thriller set on Holy Island featuring the Lindisfarne Gospels. Cynthia sighs and stands up; time to lay the table. She takes her notebook and pen from her sewing cupboard and puts the sherry bottle and two glasses out on place mats. As she is tipping a packet of cashews into a glass dish, the doorbell rings. She drops the empty packet and hurries to the door.

'Miriam, you're early!'

Miriam, wearing her red woolly coat with the collar turned up, steps into the hallway. With unrestrained delight, Cynthia reaches out and runs her hand down Miriam's sleeve, a sensuous, unconscious act of pleasure.

'I know, it reminds you of Burnham.' There's a catch in Miriam's voice and she coughs. Slipping her coat off, she hands it to Cynthia.

'The sea wall at Burnham, yes, that's where we were! I was just thinking about it, but couldn't recall the name of the place. Yes, your red coat, of course it reminds me! It was a wonderful weekend.' Cynthia tucks the coat under her chin and smiles at Miriam. She wears a black cashmere cardigan over a white cotton blouse. Cynthia's gift, a gold locket hangs around her neck. Dark charcoal-grey trousers, spun with a fine silver brocade hang from her hips. Her ash-blond hair, still like baby fluff, but getting thicker now, is swept off her forehead and tucked behind her ears, emphasising her heart-shaped face, her fine nose.

'Come here.' Cynthia hangs the coat over the bannisters and takes Miriam in her arms, breathing in her musky scent. 'God I've missed you.' She kisses her cheek.

'Don't.' Miriam wriggles away from Cynthia's embrace and walks into the dining room. She takes her usual place at the table and pours two generous measures of sherry, her hand trembles as she brings the glass to her lips and takes several sips.

Cynthia closes the door and leans against it, fiddling with the amber beads around her neck. She watches Miriam refill her glass. What to do? She knows Miriam too well to push her, to enquire. She suspects the weeks of chemotherapy have taken their toll. Was there something Miriam wasn't telling her? Miriam's treatment was four months ago and her oncologist was pleased with the results. It was all positive. Perhaps then, it was her own fears and guilt she was sensing. After all, she knows all about transference in the room. She's confident if Miriam agrees to a reading today, then whatever is hovering in the air, for both of them, will come out in the cards. She walks to her sewing desk, opens the drawer and, without hesitating, chooses The Gendron from one of many decks she'd acquired since learning the tarot.

'Shall we?' Cynthia sits down opposite Miriam, places the cards on the table between them and reaches for Miriam's hand. It feels cold, the skin dry and thin. 'Are you warm enough? I can put the fire on if you like.'

Miriam ignores the question, pulls her hand away, picks up the cards and fans them on the table. 'The tarot. That's your answer to everything isn't it?'

'I think it helps. It has before, hasn't it?'

'That was when I was well. I'm sick Cynthia. Look at me.'

'But the chemo, the Arimidex, they're working aren't they? You said ...'

'Yes, they're working. So I'm told.' Miriam shuffles the cards with care. 'I'm tired, that's all. It doesn't matter. I'd rather not talk about it. Shall we begin?'

Cynthia nods and settles in her chair, adjusting her beads, taking a sip of her sherry, noticing her shoulders relaxing. 'Yes, let's. Split the cards Miriam and, as you do so, ask yourself the question what is it I am curious about today? Don't force anything, just see what comes up. Take your time, Sweet.'

Miriam's eyelashes flutter; her tiny, stubby lashes she'd taken care to blacken with mascara. Cynthia's tummy clenches and her eyes prick with tears. She looks away and considers the question for herself. She stares out of the window to the trees at the bottom of the garden, their leaves falling, disappearing into a carpet of bronze and yellow. She decides she's curious about endings and new beginnings. What would Gerald do if she told him? Would he already know? If she explained it all, would he understand?

'I'm ready,' Miriam murmurs.

Cynthia turns back to the table. Miriam has split the pack into three. Her cheeks are flushed. Cynthia reaches across the table and pats Miriam's hand. 'Turn them over, Sweet, as you tell me. Tell me what you're curious about today, now, in this moment.'

'I want to know,' Miriam begins, 'I want to know what it's like for you?' Miriam meets Cynthia's eye. She turns over a card from the first pile – the justice card.

Cynthia scribbles: 'balance', 'true', 'karma' and 'listening' in her notebook and takes a sip of sherry. She waits for Miriam to go on.

'I want to know what you dream about and why.'

Cynthia nods encouragement.

Miriam takes a card from the second pile. She holds it so only she can see it. She frowns, dips her head, places the card face down on the table and slides it towards Cynthia.

Cynthia picks it up. A tiny hiccup escapes from the back of her throat. The prince of cups. She writes: 'exhaustion', 'homecoming', 'celebration' and puts her pen down. 'Go on Sweet, one more.'

Miriam looks up, meets her eye. 'And why, when you know what I know ...' Miriam takes a card from the third pile and snaps it, face up, onto the table. 'Why is it you don't leave him?'

They both stare at the card. The lovers. Cynthia picks up her pen, her hand shakes as she writes: 'sacrifice', 'Miriam', 'crossroads', 'Gerald', 'betray?' She closes her notebook and puts her pen down.

*

Simple pleasures help the long days pass. Taking tea with herself has become part of Cynthia's daily routine, timed exactly to the moment the afternoon play begins on the radio. So it is today, as yesterday, Cynthia opens the door to her dining room to begin preparations. She pauses to delight in the sunshine falling through the French windows, striking the mahogany sideboard and lighting up the bureau. The writing desk is a new purchase, and stands where her sewing desk used to be. Cynthia no longer needs it. She puts the tray with her best china teapot, cup and saucer, matching milk jug and sugar bowl on the table along with a selection of teatime biscuits. Soft voices, not listened to, emanate from the radio – the afternoon play has begun.

Cynthia is alone in her dining room. She waits for no one.

CHARLIE'S STORY

Peter Hardinge

Very little was known about Charlie. He always sat at the table nearest the fire in the local pub. The pub was nothing special, but it was the hub of the council estate, built at the same time as the neighbouring houses, the statutory church, newsagent and the Co-op in the 1950s when the state housing boom coincided with the baby boom after the war. Inside the pub it looked as tired as some of the clientele, their faces marked with their own versions of history to the point where you felt curious and wanted to ask them their stories.

Charlie was one of those. He always sat there, no matter what the season, drinking from his own pint mug and always the weakest real ale available of which he could drink copious amounts. Charlie was a wiry man with short grey hair cut to military style length; a short back and sides I believe they called it? Charlie wasn't a local. You could tell by his high cheekbones, his bone structure, which gave away his eastern European origins, and of course his very slightly accented English when drunk. He was a mixture of east meets west. To most of us Charlie was a mystery, hobbling around on one leg, but he never ever complained. He wasn't a local; his accent most certainly gave that away on those rare occasions but he was accepted like so many who had moved into the area as refugees. He was always stoic. You could feel that it was a trait that had been nurtured from extremes of experience, something un-English, something inherited from his eastern European culture. At times he had been the victim of the pub adolescents mocking his accent – using his pub nickname Czech Point Charlie. Of course the youthful mob thought they knew everything about Czech Point Charlie but he took little notice. He had experienced far worse during the war. He sent a smile their way along with strongly accented wise words that diffused the potential for a situation to occur, his accent fueling the laughter. 'Why you talk me like this?' he would respond purposely in broken English; his real English accent was as English as a BBC presenter from the 1940s. Charlie was protected by the pub customers as a whole – those who knew their history – and the youngsters knew that they should tread very carefully *never* daring to venture into even mild racism.

Charlie also had other talents. He was also exceptionally gifted in maths, and could play the violin. I often thought of the people from the east being more adept with music. I guess we all have the ability but we don't, in the west, always have either the pushy parents or the same peer pressure applied to be enabled with a musical instrument. Come to that, we didn't have the money for the instrument either … but I digress. Charlie had always been there whenever you entered the pub. He was one of those certainties that provides security by his presence a little like the queen; just there. I had been divorced, of which he had no personal experience, but he was just always there beside you if you needed him to be. He would quietly listen – a father figure. You also knew, when talking your problems through with Charlie that they didn't come close to the life-threatening situation that drove him across Europe to be here. This gave me perspective on my problems.

So when he was missing on that Tuesday night, I noticed it but thought nothing of it. Was he just ill? I thought perhaps he had a cold. I should perhaps go and see him. He still wasn't there two days later when I came to the pub. I thought about my previous conversations with Charlie which had centred on his history; his experiences which, as an avid history lover, I found fascinating. I had vetted his story for gaps when I first met him and checked his facts in that way we all do to ensure stories are true. They all seemed to be genuine which earned him my respect. Charlie had been born just in time for war, growing up in that one-of-many archaic eras which guaranteed you your place in history and when you would have heard of obscure places such as Catalonia, Guernica and Monte Casino, appreciative of their respective places in history. So our chats, at times, would settle on those distant places and their political significance in the twentieth century.

Charlie's own history had also been significant and fascinating. As an orphan, he had made the journey west by becoming a stowaway, somehow managing not to get deported by joining the navy in that chaotic sequence prior to war. Shortly after joining, he lost a limb, his right leg, to a German shell that had skidded across a wet deck in the North Sea. He even mentioned that the shell came in on the port side during the attack. The detail of the sea battle fascinated me. You could easily picture the long-range shoot-outs between ships miles from each other. His storytelling took you to the day, the event and to the outcome. I was amazed the way he felt no animosity to those who had fired the shell. In fact I could imagine Charlie shaking the hand of the man responsible, explaining it was just war.

Charlie had married after the war and had two children but was himself an orphan before he left the east. He could offer no information about his past beyond the local Czech orphanage where he was raised. Charlie, real name Karol, always met you with a twinkle in his eye and a humorous, 'No thanks you not for me.' This always made me smile as I knew he would refuse the pint were it on offer. 'I no drink,' he would say with an unshaven smile on his face. Charlie had been ill suffering heart problems – angina and had been missing from the pub for some time, until he decided that he would rather be happy – smoking and drinking at the pub, rather than being, in his words, 'healthy and lonely at home.' His children had left home some time ago; both were married. His wife had died two years previously so home was a solitary place. He would often ask me, when he saw me, to come round during the stay-at-home period.

I did visit him at home but I didn't do it enough. You just never seem to when the only reason for doing so is the other person's loneliness. Charlie would ask on these visits, straying into accented English, 'How's is pub?' How is this and how is that? Questions about his pub mates were always met with, 'They're OK.'

I wanted to get him out of the house, out of the pub habit so when I suggested, 'How about a walk, Charlie? It will do us good – be good for your heart. Perhaps aim for a daily target together? I'll help. What do you say?' The look said it all and the response, 'Won't do me any good now,' indicated to me that the towel was being thrown in. Not giving in, I suggested, 'Come on Charlie. Please. Moping here is no good,' but I daren't say, 'Moping about your wife won't bring her back either,' because I knew he would break down – or worse – get angry. Now I wish I had said the words, as someone needed to hit a nerve to make him turn a corner and make him realise what he had; and not fixate on what he didn't have. With two kids and numerous grandchildren, his wife, I imagined, would be angry if she were here. So to pull him away from his ceaseless spiralling journey downwards, to break the negativity, the walk became a walk to the pub.

It was a warm summer evening. Charlie's smile, which increased as we set off, grew as we got closer. He was a lost cause who knew his days were numbered and, despite it all, knew where his last days should be spent. They weren't going to be moping at home or starting an exercise plan to prolong a life he knew was drawing to an end. Or as he put it humorously, 'giving up cigarettes and prolonging the agony of his existence.' Yes, he had also learnt the English sense of humour!

So Charlie's walk – I thought walk of shame, for him was like walking home after an unwanted and extended period of time away. I had called in advance to tell Steve the landlord the likely outcome of the afternoon and that we may turn up at the pub. Steve in his certainty of the outcome, unlike me, had it planned with sandwiches. He knew Charlie wouldn't have eaten all day, which was a testament to knowing his customers. It was for the best. Who knows how much longer you'll have when you're just plain and simple happy? Happy and being with those you see as close friends, communicating, having fun, just enjoying company; feeling 'with' rather than feeling 'without'.

The afternoon turned into a beautiful, mild, summer evening; swallows relentlessly flying back and forth, with the sun making its slow journey downward to be replaced by its sister the moon. Plates of sandwiches were being handed out to everyone so Charlie didn't feel it was just for him. Despite my best efforts he must have been aware of my forward plans, the call to Steve, to get Charlie out of his downward journey.

For some time after, Charlie picked up the thread he had again created, and now continued with the daily journey to the pub – on the way to the newsagent's to collect his daily portion of cigarettes. 'You won't live to a ripe old age if you keep the smoking up,' I smiled. To my surprise, he smiled back and said that may be the point. So I watched helplessly as I knew it futile to discuss his now slow slide towards the inevitable. I did however contact his daughter, asking her to surprise him with a visit but not to mention I'd called. I waited for him to break the news about the visit but he said nothing. So had she turned up with the grandkids?

To my amazement, the whole family turned up at the pub, feigned surprise not to find him at the house and so decided to come for a drink with the kids in the beer garden. While the kids played, Charlie was talking to both his son and daughter about his journey to the UK, the reasons why he came, and why he wanted now to go back to 'follow his tracks,' was how he put it. His children Jan and Sophie listened intently, as did I, when he talked of the long walk, stealing rides in the back of lorries and scavenging food. All he knew was that he wanted to go west so he followed the direction, eventually becoming a stowaway in France and jumping ship to London in late 1938. His timing was impeccable as he had managed to go through Nazi Germany, avoiding the UK border control, and work without the correct documentation right up to the beginning of the war. Charlie said that when war broke out, it was his duty and privilege to join the UK Navy to fight fascism. He said he was too late to get to Spain but not too late to fight in the war of good against evil. The words were spat out with true venom. To me there was more to the statement than speaking passionately after a few beers. Sophie asked Charlie, 'You OK, Dad?' The children continued playing as Charlie revealed that his, and subsequently their, surname was Dormitzer and not Dormiczech. We all looked at him, not taking in the significance of the statement. As we carried on staring at Charlie for the answer, he just said, 'It's a Jewish name. For years I've hidden this but never felt like revealing it'. Jan asked, 'Why reveal this now?' Both Jan and Sophie didn't look shocked, more surprised. It's not every day you discover your Jewish roots! 'It is time,' Charlie said, 'to recognise what little I know of my past and to pass this onto the two most important people in my life.' He continued, 'If I had stayed in my country, I faced certain death but I survived by moving here. I am fortunate; one, that I made it here – many did not – and two, to have brought you children into this world to continue life's cycle by passing on my love and the wealth of my being. You will now pass this on to your children and I will be a happy man knowing that.' He added, staring into the distance: 'By saving a soul, you save the world.' My mind wandered into that dark period of history momentarily, knowing some of the terror but none of the fear of being Jewish and being trapped within eastern Europe.

Charlie didn't make the pub the next night, and now that night had felt like a goodbye. It had been a lovely evening; the grand kids playing with granddad and Charlie's grown up children just being there with him. That feeling of cross sentiment, of well-being with no words needing to be said – just being in each other's company – was enough. The word was family and love.

AT ANY AGE
A PLAY SCRIPT

Kathryn B Hollingworth

INTERNAL. KITCHEN - DAY

JAMES (8) sits on a stool at the kitchen table drinking a glass of lemonade.

STAN (78) sits beside James and is drinking from a mug of tea.

> JAMES
> I wish I was old like you,
> Grandpa.

> STAN
> Why?

> JAMES
> Because I wouldn't have to go to
> school.

> STAN
> Yes, but there would be lots of other things that you
> didn't like, that you would have to do.

> JAMES
> Like what, Grandpa?

> STAN
> You may have to climb the stairs
> with creaky knees and take heart
> pills every day.

James takes a sip of his lemonade.

> STAN (CONT'D)
> I'm not going to lecture you about the importance
> of going to school and getting an education, as the
> most important things I've learned about in life, I
> didn't find out about at school.

Stan smiles wryly and takes a drink from his mug.

> STAN (CONT'D)
> But tell me somethin' James, why
> don't you like school?

> JAMES
> Because there's a mean teacher and bullies there.

> STAN
> There's bullies everywhere, James. If you learn to
> stand up to 'em when you're young it'll be a lot
> easier later on. Take my next-door neighbour for
> instance. He throws weeds on my lawn and yells at
> me every time I go outside to my car. He's a bully if
> ever I saw one.

James looks thoughtful as he gulps down more of his lemonade.

> JAMES
> It's hard at school. You have to
> do hard stuff like maths and
> writing.

> STAN
> I find writing hard as I've got
> arthritis in these old mitts.

Stan looks down briefly at his hands.

> STAN (CONT'D)
> And I've never found doing sums easy, especially
> nowadays. All of those numbers keep on getting
> muddled in my head. Tell you what, I've still got my
> old motorboat. Why don't you and I take it out on
> the river this afternoon?

James looks excited and jumps down from the stool.

                    JAMES
          That'd be great, Grandpa. We can
          be pirates or explorers.

                    STAN
          It'll be fun. After all, you can go on adventures at
          any age.

GETTING THE BLUES

Gill Wilson

Phil pointed to the noticeboard. 'That's not good Kathy,' he said. 'Nobody I know has ever benefited from this kind of interference.' 'You old cynic,' I say.

> *There is a meeting in the conference room 16.40 today*
> *with Morag from Human Resources. Please arrive promptly.*
> *Jim*

This job has been a large part of my life. For twenty five years I have been with the company; ever since leaving school. It's provided the success that eluded me in my childhood, reassuring me that I did, in fact, have something of value to offer. When things at home were turbulent, the job kept me sane.

'We are planning a "dress down Friday" this week,' smiles Morag at the start of the meeting. 'And we've got a few things organised so that we can have a little fun and do some team building.'

'What for?' says Phil. 'We're already a good team.'

'Well … we're going to ask each of you to complete a questionnaire, looking at your individual personality types. Each one has a different colour: orange, green, blue and gold. There aren't any right or wrong answers,' she says. 'We want to bring out the best in everybody. It is more efficient for the company if you engage with colleagues who complement your methods of working.'

'Not me. I don't like that kind of psychobabble. I think it's dangerous. What happens if we have too many people with the blues?' says Phil.

'Wouldn't you like to know what colour you are?' says Morag in a tone usually reserved for five-year-olds.

'No,' says Phil.

Morag is an overweight woman in her late forties who strides through the office at regular intervals, wearing flamboyant clothes more suited to Ladies Day at Ascot than the office. She has an unapproachable air. Sitting in a room with her is like waiting in the dentist's chair for a root canal filling.

The jeans worn by most of us on the Friday, accentuate Morag's new floral affair as it attempts to hide her hefty legs.

'Flexible … organised … compassionate … versatile …' repeats Morag. 'Which one comes first?'

I chew my nails. 'Can't I be all of those?' I say.

'Yes … but which is the *most* like you? Put them in order of importance. Quick, quick. It's meant to be spontaneous.' Her exasperation isn't helping.

'Compassionate … err … flexible, versatile … and organised,'

'What do you think Phil would have put for that one?' says Morag.

'What? I don't know. I wouldn't want to answer on his behalf,' I say. 'Surely it is up to him if he wants to let you know how he feels.' She frowns, and looks back at her clipboard.

Colours are duly assigned to employees - apart from Phil.

'I see they've put our colours on the noticeboard,' I say to Phil.

'I hope they've not chosen one for me.'

'No. But I bet they are counting you as black.'

'Oh good,' he says. 'I like the sound of that.'

Morag seems to be around more; huddled together with Jim for hours at a time. In the main office, keyboards are tap-tapping alongside subdued voices. One of the conference rooms becomes the venue for the new Monday morning briefings. It is a room where the neutral grey colour of the carpet creeps up the walls to the ceiling. White vertical blinds adorn the small window. My eyes are drawn to the functional-looking, white, analogue clock. Its loud tick fills the room with anticipation as we wait for the meeting to start. With only a few chairs in the room, most of us are standing. We shuffle forwards making space for Phil as he walks into the room and shivers. Morag looks at her watch, sighs and makes her announcement:

'I am sorry to have to tell you that we have been discussing the downsizing of the business. Sadly, this is the only way that we can prevent the company from failing altogether. By going through this painful process we can, at least, protect some of our jobs. Everything that we decide will be open and transparent.'

'You can almost see the fork in her tongue,' whispers Rachel. Morag glares in her direction.

'That reminds me,' she says. 'You will notice, in the main office, that the coffee machine has been moved. There is no longer any room to linger by the machine so you need to take the coffee to your desk.'

'There is far too much non-work related chatter taking place in this building,' adds Jim.

Within a week, performance management meetings are arranged, targets set and capability measured. One by one, we are called into the chilly conference room for an individual face-to-face meeting with Morag. This has all been so fast.

'Well, Kathy?' says Morag. 'What do you think of the targets you have been set?'

'I think they are unachievable,' I say, sitting upright in my chair. 'They are woolly ... open to interpretation. Is that your intention?' I am becoming more outspoken now that I feel cornered. Perhaps I can go back to my colour test and change my answers: loyal and dependable can become challenging and confrontational. After a few others have been to their meetings, a pattern begins to form: if you are old enough to be well paid but too young to be pensioned off, you are the most vulnerable.

The monologues from Morag make the briefings increasingly sombre affairs. Comments are not welcome and any contributions are generally ridiculed.

'I wish she would send out an email instead of all this grandstanding,' says Phil.

'But it would spoil her fun. She wants us to feel the malevolence ... not delete her.'

In one of these meetings, as I sit there with words tumbling around me, thinking about the shopping I need to get on the way home, I feel pressure on my arm. Rachel is sitting beside me looking straight ahead at Morag. Her eyes widen to encourage me to follow her gaze. The brightly coloured top that Morag is wearing has rolled up, revealing a vast expanse of flabby, white, dimpled flesh. The quiet around me is not the usual bored silence but is vibrant and alert. My skin prickles as if flirting with nettles. Everyone is staring straight ahead like mannequins in a shop window not daring to exchange glances. This electrifying moment changes the mood for the whole day. There is a bounce in the air; knowing smirks are exchanged.

'I just wish that I could have been there when Morag noticed her wardrobe malfunction,' says Rachel at the end of the day. 'I'd love to have seen the expression on her face as she tried to work out exactly when it happened, and who might have seen it.'

'EVERYBODY Morag!' we giggle.

*

Several desks stand empty. Kaleb, from accounts has not been seen for a few days and we assume that he has left, silenced by a confidentiality clause. When Phil comes out of Jim's office slamming the door so hard that the glass cracks, it makes me jump. He marches to his desk and starts throwing his personal things into a box with Morag standing beside him.

'Sorry guys,' he says. 'I would love to say goodbye but according to Her Lardyship, I am not allowed to talk to any of you!' As he walks towards the door, he lands a direct kick at the water machine.

'That's it!' I say to Rachel as we walk home. 'Tonight I start looking for a new job. This place is killing me. Honestly, I can feel the years falling away. I am so wound up … all the time.'

*

I look up at the smart new office block as I arrive for my first interview in twenty five years.

'Well Kathy,' says the smart young woman. 'I like what I see on your résumé. Your references are glowing. I think that you would fit in very well here.' I smile and take a breath.

'I notice that your reference is from your previous employer. I will need to ask for one from your current boss, even though he is fairly new. I'm sure that won't be a problem for you.'

'You look rough!' says Rachel as I wander into the office the next morning. 'You didn't get it then? I'm so sorry.'

'Actually I did,' I say. 'But I've got to ask Jim for a reference! What are the chances … with Morag looking over his shoulder?'

'Ohh … rather you than me,' says Rachel. I should wait until Old Lardy comes out of Jim's office. Don't let her hear that you've gone and got yourself a job. Only she can decide who stays and who goes.'

I'm sure that it's illegal to write a bad reference. Anyway, whatever the outcome, I can't stay here. As few of us are being asked to give any notice, I can be out of here by the end of the week.

I catch a glimpse of the balloons and streamers being smuggled in for my 'surprise' party. I am delighted to be leaving on my own terms and I can smell the freedom on the other side of the main door as I walk towards it with my box of possessions. The phone on my desk rings, calling me back one last time. It's about the new job …

As I sling the box in the boot of my car, Rachel appears.

'We're all waiting for you,' she smiles. 'I know that you've sussed what we're doing. I'm gasping for a glass of something. And wait 'til you see the cake!' She steps away from me as I lift my head. Tears stream down my hot cheeks.

'I'm not coming,' I say. 'Please go and enjoy my party. But I want you to ask that bitch what it was she and Jim did to lose me my new job.'

*

Gradually, those of us who have escaped, create a kind of informal support group. We meet for a walk or a coffee or an early evening pizza. Others, still in the office, fighting for their own survival, decline our invitations; the management does not approve of such fraternizing. They are happy to abandon us in their own fights for survival.

It takes several weeks of talking about little other than 'Her Lardyship' and the injustices of our plight before we start to move on and enjoy one another's company. The weather improves as we move into summer and with it our moods. Sally gets a part-time job with less money and a lot less stress. Parveen lands the job of her dreams which she would have never dared apply for a year ago. Rachel is doing the paperwork for her self-employed husband and Phil is playing more bridge and embracing his new role of Granddad. Wounds are healing.

*

'So what are you going to do Mum?' my daughter asks. 'You know that my place is looking for an office manager. I think it would really suit you.'

'Oh, I don't know … I think that I'm done with office culture.'

'I'll email you the ad. I can certainly help you to get an interview but the rest is up to you.' My daughter has always had a gift for timing and senses that I'm getting restless. I need to feel productive again.

Jackson's is a large company that has somehow managed to keep the personal touch of its humble beginnings. Richard, the boss, was pleased that I could start straight away. There is a lot to do but I am well supported and I feel appreciated. I'd forgotten what it's like to be thanked for simply doing my job. Richard has the foresight to know that a full lunch hour, decent coffee breaks and a flexible attitude towards working hours means that everyone is relaxed and committed to the firm. The offices are sunny, where you can breathe in the fresh air and feel alive.

As I am chased in through the door by a flurry of amber leaves on a beautiful, crisp morning, I notice that the door of Richard's office is closed. I sit down at my desk and the phone rings. Richard asks me to bring my notebook and sit in on an interview. This is not part of my job description but I'm happy to help.

'Can I get anyone a coffee?' I ask.

'No thanks,' says Richard. 'Ms Briggs?'

I look closely, recognising the name, and there is Morag sitting the other side of his desk. I hold onto a chair as my legs start to buckle. I feel sick.

'Ms Briggs? Coffee?' repeats Richard, raising his voice with an edge of impatience.

She shakes her head, a polite smile vanishing. I can imagine her flabby stomach knotting and, as my heart beat returns to normal, I feel relaxed. Richard indicates the chair where he would like me to sit. It forms a barrier between Morag and the door, and has been placed slightly behind her. I can see her clearly but she cannot see me without turning her head.

'To recap, Ms Briggs,' says Richard. 'This is a large company with small origins. Our success is in not forgetting how we started and how hard my father and his sister worked to get it to where it is today.' She nods. Red patches have formed around her neck and ample bosom.

'We need a team player; someone who has an overview of the staff and their well-being. I see human resources as a link between management and staff. If the workforce feels appreciated, the company will run smoothly.

Wouldn't you agree?' Richard stares at her. She looks at the floor. 'You told me that you feel the same; that in your previous HR role, the well-being of your colleagues was of paramount importance to you; and you did all you could to support them.'

'Er ... Yes. I did.'

'If people are unhappy, feel unfulfilled or unimportant, they will disengage from the success of the company. Won't they, Ms Briggs?'

'Yes ... of course ... '

The red patch travels upwards, covering Morag's face. Her podgy fingers reach for the jug on the table, spilling water as she tries to fill a glass.

'Then I'm sure you will agree, Ms Briggs, that the role of Human Resources Manager is one of great integrity?'

'Yes.'

'Tell me,' Richard says, apparently unaware of Morag's discomfort, 'why did you leave your last position?' He pauses. 'I gather from your application that you were made redundant three months ago.'

'That's correct.'

'But I don't understand why, for someone in such a senior position, your references are so non-committal. There is nothing here to encourage me to employ you. I can only imagine that you became surplus to requirements after you had achieved such a wonderful job with your downsizing operation.'

As Morag starts to formulate an answer, Richard gets to his feet and holds out his hand. She pushes herself out of the chair and takes his hand, wincing at the firm grip.

'Thank you for coming in today. You will be hearing from us soon.'

'You look a little red, Morag,' I blurt out. 'Is that something to do with your personality type?'

Morag avoids looking at me as she stumbles to the door.

'Thank you for sitting in,' Richard says. 'I thought that you might be interested in today's interview.'

I am still shocked by my outburst. I try to apologise.

'By the way,' says Richard, 'when you next see Phil for a pizza, you can let him know that Her Lardyship did not do well in her interview and is not going to be offered the post.'

He whistles as he walks back to his office. 'Good. That was nice and quick,' he says, 'and I always try to get away a little early on bridge night.'

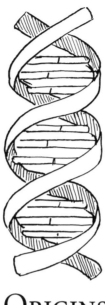

ORIGINS

Anasua Sarkar Roy

She died on a crisp January morning. A gap in the curtains let in a beam of light. I sat next to her bed holding her hand whilst Dad held mine. He never spoke to me in the same way after that morning.

'This is for you, Reynolds. You need to read this on your own,' he said, as he handed me an envelope with my name in Mum's handwriting. He retreated into his study whilst I opened the letter. I read the first sentence.

'You are my son,' she wrote, 'but you're not my genetic son.'

What did she mean? I felt dizzy. I took a few deep breaths and resisted the urge to walk towards Dad's study. Instead, I walked up to my old bedroom and lay in bed, under my covers, with my head propped up by pillows. I felt comforted by the surrounding familiarity and continued reading her letter.

'I love you more than words can say but I could never find the courage to tell you. It was never the right time. I almost told you on your eighteenth birthday but by then I had chosen the easier path. My greatest fear was you'd be angry with me for keeping this secret from you. By the time I'd decided to tell you the truth, I couldn't risk it. Love and fear are so closely related. Before you were born, I was so angry with my situation. I felt so helpless. It nearly destroyed me from within. I don't want you to feel the same way as you read these words. In those days, I resented any woman who held a baby in their arms because I so wanted one of my own. When I finally held you in my arms, it felt like you were mine forever. Except, that isn't what being a mother is about. As the years passed, I realised that your child is never really yours. They are in the world because of you, but not owned by you.'

I remembered I had to take a swab from both my parents for an experiment in my undergraduate days. I never managed to get Mum's swab.

'This letter felt so wrong to your dad. He always said that one of us should tell you face to face. I insisted that I couldn't do that. I'd never have told you, but the IVF clinic wrote to me about your egg donor. She left her contact details which I have included in the last page of this letter. I called her and asked her to wait until I recovered to contact her back. I never did. Your dad was so close to telling you, but I stopped him. It was my fear and not his. Please understand this and don't judge him.'

The first page ended there. I wasn't sure how I felt about Dad. He had a choice long before Mum became ill. I turned to the final page.

'In those days, donors could stay anonymous and that's what she chose until three years ago, around the time my cancer treatment started. The letter from the IVF clinic was submitted by the egg donor to the HFEA and that's how they got in touch with us. Your dad and I argued about letting you know about her, but I was scared of losing you and we kept putting things off. He agreed to go along with my wishes until the very end. Forgive us and try to understand. I know now, the right time to tell a secret is to tell it before it becomes one.

We both love you more than life itself.'

*

Every Sunday morning, we would cook a huge meal together. Before all our friends arrived, the three of us would sit perched on the bar stools around the large central island, peeling onions, garlic and ginger, chopping and slicing vegetables and drinking coffee. Dad forgot to take his Metformin that morning and jumped off his stool.

'I can't believe I've got to take these pills every day. No one has diabetes in my family.' Dad ran five kilometres every day and believed he would be able to go through life without any biochemical intervention.

'Yeah, but I bet they didn't eat as many puddings as you did.' I laughed and Mum raised an eyebrow and continued slicing the onions for the soup.

'You have a point.' He nodded and paused to swallow his pill. 'It's all about what you absorb into your body from food and the environment, and these trigger chain reactions that cause disease. Genetically we're all pretty similar.' He spoke as he walked to fetch the bowl of custard from the fridge and then returned to sit on his stool. 'Hmm,' he said as he looked up from the recipe book, 'have you decided what postgraduate course you're going to go for?' It was unlike Dad to change the subject so quickly.

'Hold on! What's the point of the whole genome project if it's all down to our environment? I thought you were more scientific than that?'

'Just because scientists believe in something doesn't make it scientific.' He looked up to see my expression and suppressed a smile before he replied. 'Identifying the human genome is just the first spoon of the pudding but using this to find out more about how the environment affects us is the rest of it.' He chuckled as he ladled the custard into the trifle.

'Pudding?' I laughed. 'What about my perfect pitch inherited from Mum?' I smiled at Mum waiting for her to stride in with a comment.

'Practice makes perfect; not genes,' she said.

'Maybe it's your genes that allow you to become what you are,' I said.

'But not who you are ... right?' she said emphatically looking at Dad. Then the doorbell rang.

*

It was Dad's birthday a week ago and he hasn't opened his letters and cards that I placed on the kitchen island from last Sunday. I visit Dad every weekend, since Mum died two months ago. I try to talk to him, but he refuses help. If he won't speak to me about the letter, then I need to make a decision on whether to contact her. I keep Mum's letter in my wallet. I take out the letter, unfold the familiar creases and focus directly on the phone number, with the name JOSEPHINE BEACON written carefully next to it. This time, I call her. She answers.

'Hello, Josephine Beacon speaking.' Her voice sounds assured and business like. I fight the urge to hang up.

'Hello, I'm Reynolds Motha, Isabella's son.'

'Oh yes. How lovely. Isabella promised me your father would call me after she ... I lost my husband three years ago, so I can understand what he must be going through.'

'Can we meet?' The words just escape from my mouth.

There is a pause. 'Of course. I'm at home most of the time.'

'Tomorrow after three in the afternoon?'

'Tomorrow?' She sounds surprised. 'Yes. That suits me.'

'Great. I'll see you at three-thirty.'

*

The gravel driveway circled round a well-kept, perfect lawn. The daffodils lining the driveway swayed. Yellow, Mum's favourite colour. A red moped rested next to the steps leading up to the door, framed by two regal-looking, white pillars. From my car, I could see that it had two large Georgian windows either side of the front door. As I walked towards the front door, a man smiled and nodded from above the hedge surrounding the house which he was trimming.

I knocked. The door was opened promptly by a woman in her thirties. She was wearing a tailored dress with a suede jacket and a saddlebag hooked over her shoulder.

'Hello, I'm Reynolds. Mrs Beacon is expecting me.'

'Of course!' She relaxed and opened the door wider. 'I'm Emily. Please come in. Mother said you're visiting her today.'

I followed her in to the house. The hallway opened in to a large living area with dark wooden floors and white walls. In the corner, I noticed a Steinway grand piano and I paused to look at it.

'Mother's piano. Do you play?'

'Not on a piano like that. You?'

'No way. Nor my brother Mark. Maybe you can play something after I get back?' she sighed.

I smiled and nodded then continued to follow her. The light was flooding in from the skylights above. As the room narrowed, I noticed a window ledge covered with large sea shells. My fiancé, Uma, had a similar collection she had dotted around our apartment, next to photographs of her family in Mauritius.

'Reynolds is an unusual first name?' Emily was leading me through to a closed door.

'People think it's my surname. It has something to do with fluid flow mechanics. Names say more about our parents than us.' I looked back at Emily as she paused to face me.

152

'Yes. I suppose so. Emily and Mark are quite traditional names.' Emily opened a heavy-looking door. 'And this,' she made an exaggerated flurrying gesture with her hands and put on a posh accent, 'is the library.'

My eyes had to adjust to the darkness of the room. I saw the forearms of a woman with her back to me sitting on an upright armchair. Two sides of the room were filled with shelves full of books. An empty armchair faced hers and a round table in between with a tray of things covered by a tea towel.

'Mother. This is Reynolds.' Emily waited while the woman stood up to face me as I walked towards her.

'Thank you for waiting Emily and showing Reynolds in.'

'I'll leave you both to talk. I'm running late.' Emily closed the door behind her.

Josephine Beacon held her right hand outstretched ready to shake hands with me. 'Hello Reynolds. I've been looking forward to meeting you.' Her hand felt cold. She gestured to the chair next to hers. The room looked cluttered and old fashioned compared to the other part of the house. It had a pleasant smell of spring; not the musty smell of books as I had expected it would. The one, small window was left open. She looked pale and delicate and, despite her dark hair, looked much older than I had calculated.

'Would you like some tea and fruit cake?'

'Thank you.' I heard the sound of a moped starting up outside. As I waited, I noticed an oil painting of a castle above the fireplace and the mantlepiece had an assortment of silver bells.

'This was my husband's favourite room. He loved clutter and I'm the exact opposite.' She watched me as I stood up and walked towards the fireplace.

'Quite a collection here.' I picked up the smallest bell and rang it. It startled her and I resisted an impulse to pick up another bell. I examined her face as she poured my tea. Her face looked sharp and boney, unlike mine. Some would call that kind of face attractive, but I didn't.

'Those bells were his little collection. God knows why. That oil painting you were looking at was the only painting of Mark's he liked. All the others were far too abstract for his liking.' She placed my cup on the table and started to cut a large piece of cake. 'Well, I am really glad to meet you. Tell me a bit about yourself.'

'Yes,' I paused to think. 'I'm leading a project, following on from my

PhD, in genome-scale evolutionary sequence analyses, to illuminate the function of regulatory elements and proteins. I've received sponsorship from an American research company to work with an expert team in cybernetics and link it up with the effects of ... ' I noticed the familiar expression I had seen on many faces as I looked up from stirring my tea. 'Sorry,' I shrugged. 'I can get carried away.'

'Passion is never a bad thing. It's finding what makes one passionate. That is the real challenge.' She placed the plate with fruitcake alongside my cup. 'I play the piano. Emily's passionate about being a paediatrician and Mark is an artist.' She paused to look at my face intently. I think she was smiling.

'I used to play the piano.' I felt guilty and irritated. I wish I had practiced. Those times arguing with my mum seemed so wasteful. 'Mum nearly had a career as a musician, but she decided to teach music at my primary school.'

'What a waste! Being a musician is a rare gift that needs nurturing. I used to have an international career as a classical concert pianist.' As she looked down at her hands, I noticed they were shaking. 'I have Parkinson's. Idiopathic or is it idiotpathic causes, so Emily says. It probably had to do with not having Arnold alongside me. I think it was the sadness of losing him ... or, I'm finally getting old?'

'Was that around the time you wanted Mum to contact you?'

'Yes. When Isabella responded, I knew it was the right decision.'

'Did Mum ever meet you?'

'No. It was about you. Not us.'

I turned my head to look out of the window, at the field and horizon. The sun had disappeared behind clouds as the room darkened. I got up to close the window. She switched on a lamp beside her.

'Look! How wonderful. A rainbow. Always a good sign.' We admired the rainbow over the field; underneath a horse was galloping. The view looked like a clichéd country painting. 'That horse doesn't belong to us. We just rent the land out.'

'Oh,' I nodded. I had an overwhelming feeling of loss gushing through me. I longed to find Mum and tell her I didn't care about my genetic origins. She wouldn't have wasted time in torment.

'You know, Arnold didn't want me to do it. It was a miracle I had so many healthy eggs at that age. I just knew that a good deed would pay back. After that I had Emily and then fell pregnant with Mark without IVF. It's strange to think that one action like that can affect so many lives.' She stared out at the rainbow as she spoke. 'Why did you decide to meet me?'

'I was curious. Mum's letter wasn't very detailed, and I needed to know more.' I breathed out as I relaxed back into my armchair. 'What about you? Why did you want to find out about me after all these years?'

She tilted her head to one side and closed her eyes for a moment. 'I felt I was missing something in my life. I've always had that feeling inside me. It drives me to do things. Even as a little girl. It's who I am.'

'It still doesn't explain why you didn't do it before?'

'Good question. Truthfully ... I was just too busy with my own career and my own family and my world that I'd created. Then age creeps up on you. You think you've created this perfect life for yourself, but then it starts to slip away. It begins with losing those you love and parts of yourself that you love and parts of a world that you created around you that you love. You soon discover that everything you created, disappears. Even memories, in Arnold's case. He forgot who I was in the last few months of his life. He was twenty years older than me. I think I aged with him though.' Her face had softened as she turned her head to look at me. 'I suppose all this is quite difficult for you?'

'Yes. Secrets. They never work in life. Mum regretted nothing except her decision to keep the egg donation a secret all these years. Dad's emotionally detached himself from me since Mum died and I thought meeting you might make things better. Secrets, or just not telling, it's all a way of creating a life that we want for ourselves without appreciating what we have. That's all this means to me now. That one cell carrying coded information on how a body develops is not enough to decode life. Life is just living it. Maybe I just need to leave it at that.'

'Will you come back and visit again?'

I hesitated but I couldn't lie to her. 'I'm glad I met you, but it doesn't change anything for me.'

'I hope to see you again, Reynolds. It doesn't have to be about the past you know?'

'No. It doesn't. But Dad isn't leaving the past behind yet. I need to help him move forward.'

'I hope you find a way to get him back to the present.'

I nodded. I sipped my tea and ate my cake as we sat in silence for a while, looking out towards the rainbow and the horse. Dad loved cake but he stopped baking after Mum became ill. 'Do you have any recordings of your concerts online? Dad loves listening to classical piano.'

'Of course. I only have CDs of my concerts. They're in that red box next to the brass horse. Take the whole box. It's easier to carry then.'

'Thank you, Josephine. I'll come back to return these to you.'

'That would be lovely. I hope he enjoys listening to them.'

'Please don't get up. I'll see myself out.' I decided I would speak to Dad tonight rather than wait until tomorrow.

She stayed seated in her chair and looked away towards the window. I left her staring out at the rainbow that was slowly dissolving into the rain.

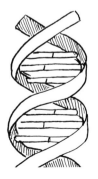

ON THE OUTSIDE

Linda Ford

I am here and no one notices
I am here and you don't see me.
In a world of youth and colour
I am here but never seen.

I speak and no one listens
I speak and you don't hear me.
In a world of noise and chatter
I speak but no one hears.

I cry and no one answers
I cry and you don't care.
In a world of exhausted emotions
I cry but no one cares.

I am alone and no one calls me
I am alone and you pass by.
In a world of social media
I am alone but no one has time.

I walk and I am a shadow
I walk but I walk alone.
In a world of constant journeys
Like a shadow I walk unknown.

LEAKING SKY

Sophie Yeomans

The place where I now live
has Father on the wall.
I turn my head to look into his eyes
and tender is the gaze returned to me.
It warms my heart and lips,
his eyes blaze blue as cerulean sky.

I feel the curving smile cross my lips,
light up my eyes,
throw blessing to the sky
when I see Grandad framed (there, up) upon the wall.
So he and they are still along with me!
Somehow by them I live.

They walk and watch the grass with me,
sap flowing lush and live,
the green cool plant floor
soothing us like sympathetic lips.
Dreaming with them, I close my eyes,
holding earth and yearning for the sky.

Out beyond the garden wall,
the wassailing angels sing for them and me.
I lean back, looking at the sky
that leaks in through my eyes
into my curdling brain, down through my lips,
to melody with things both dead and live.

Now often in my head there swims the sky
leaking out when I forget that other people's eyes
may wait to catch me, trip me up and trap me,
and words on other people's lips
conspire to close me tight behind a wall.
But I have my right, and my right way, to live!

I'm told that what I see can't open other people's eyes,
that when I speak the words mix on my lips,
that where I live has mirrors on the wall,
that I am all alone, there's only me alive,
and when I sit, I'm silent, gazing at the sky,
watching that which only comes to me.

I hold in faith, beyond the garden wall, there waits the sky.
Blessed are my eyes by those I see that live,
I move my lips and know that they hear me.

WORDSWORTH'S
FIRST DAUGHTER

Shirley Valentine Jones

It was in 1791 that William Wordsworth made his fateful trip to France. At the age of 21 he was already making a name for himself as a poet. Living in Cumberland, by the sea in Cockermouth, Wordsworth's first love was nature. His second love was Annette Vallon. This piece of writing is set in 1802 when William went again to France, with his sister Dorothy, to visit Annette for the first time in years.

'Maman – I have a papa!' Caroline jumped with joy at the thought of her very own father. 'Un papa, Maman!'

'Ssh!' her mother cautioned. 'Ssh. Don't get too excited – he's supposed to be coming from England – but that's a long way off and a hard journey. Calm down.' Annette laughed as her nine-year-old daughter ran around the small sitting room in their cottage in Calais.

It was poorly furnished and very small, but at least it was a roof over their heads. Very different from the life that Annette had been used to all those years ago when she first met William Wordsworth. That had happened in Paris ten years ago during a lull in the battles between France and England

and before the awful years at the end of the French Revolution and its Reign of Terror. They fell passionately in love. They had loved each other for the few months of William's stay, and she had conceived.

'Oh Maman – what does he look like?' asked Caroline. 'Is he handsome?'

There was so much she wanted to know. At school she had been hurt by the fact that other children had fathers and mothers and she had never known a father at all. Not even a glimpse. Her fellow scholars did not believe her when she said that her father lived in England. They had heard their mothers whispering about Annette being careless. Caroline had often come home crying from their taunts. Annette had assured her daughter that her father was a lovely handsome English poet – and that he was sure to come and join them once the state of war and revolution had ceased.

'It's not safe for him to journey here,' she said over the years whenever her daughter asked why he stayed away from them.

Two days later, a carriage drew up outside their cottage front door. A distinguished looking, rather thin man in a top hat accompanied by a well-dressed lady, got out. When the noise of the carriage had ceased, Annette opened the front door. 'Hello,' she said, almost in a whisper to William Wordsworth, looking up to the face she used to kiss.

'My dear, how long it has been? I'm so sorry I could not get to see you all these years but events made it impossible. Impossible,' he repeated as he went towards her and took her hands in his. The look in his eyes though unsettled her. He was not looking at her eyes but rather at her cheek. Not quite right somehow, she thought. She had been hoping that this would be the visit when he would declare his undying love for her and announce that they would be soon married.

Before he acknowledged his daughter who was hiding behind her mother's skirts, William introduced the lady who accompanied him. 'Annette, this is my sister Dorothy.'

Dorothy was a year younger than William. They had been baptised together and had been inseparable since childhood. As an unmarried lady, Dorothy had been taken into her brother's household and ran it for him like a wife. She also was educated and so was able to help him with some aspect of his poems and dealt with some of his business interests. This gave him more time to wander the dales and hills.

William was very interested in the philosophy behind the French Revolution but had subsequently been disillusioned by the Republican

Movement. It had been almost impossible to travel to France but he had managed to send letters and the occasional purse of money to Annette. Her home in Paris had been ransacked and she had fled to Calais to a safe place for her young daughter and herself.

'It's so good to see you William.' She turned to Dorothy. 'Both of you. Do come in. I'll get some refreshments for you after your journey. How was it?'

'Tortuous. And the channel was quite rough. But we weathered it all right. Dorothy is a real sea creature!' He turned to his sister and put his hand gently on her shoulder and bid her to go ahead into the cottage. Caroline then came out from behind her mother's skirts.

'Hello, my Papa!' she said shyly.

'Hello little girl.' William Wordsworth looked in wonder at this ginger-haired beauty, lithe of body with lovely blue-green eyes. He then smiled and said, 'Hello Caroline, I'm your father.'

'I know you are. I'm pleased that you are,' said the ingenuous nine-year-old girl. 'Are you going to stay?'

Annette stepped in quickly and told her daughter not to ask her father too many questions. 'He's tired after a long journey, which you might be making soon!' she added looking coquettishly up at William.

When they were sitting in the rather dingy room, sipping tea and having rather restrained conversation, William said to Dorothy, 'My dear, would you … could you take Caroline out for a little walk while I talk to Annette?'

Dorothy had been primed that this would happen and agreed straight away. Annette called to Caroline, 'Your Aunt wants to walk with you! Will you show her the sea front?' Caroline came out slowly from the other room and said in a low unsure voice, 'Yes, I will Maman.' She got her coat and put it on – for it was still springtime cold. William then looked at Caroline, realising that she was disappointed.

'I'm sorry little one, I myself want to see the sights later, and hope that you will come with me,' he said with a brief smile.

When Caroline and her Aunt Dorothy had left the house, William took Annette's hand. 'I would rather it was a different time and I had better news to bring you.'

Annette interrupted him. 'Dear one – I have been looking forward to you coming for so long, I can hardly believe you are here. Your letters were always welcome and made me realise that you had not forgotten me – or our daughter.'

Wordsworth coughed and fiddled with his cravat and then said, 'Letters were the only way of contact. With all the unrest and the fighting between our nations, it was impossible for me to travel to France.'

'Other friends of mine managed it!' Annette said pointedly, looking across at William. 'Not often – but they managed!'

'Maybe they had money to pay bribes!' responded William. 'Until recently I had nothing left after household bills.'

'You managed to keep your sister!' Annette said with some anger. For nine years, William had kept her waiting, vowing his love in letters.

'I am bound to look after her until she marries!' answered Wordsworth. 'It's a custom of our society.'

'It's a hope of my society that fathers honour their offspring.'

'Well now I shall, if you will allow me,' said William rather sternly.

Annette did not feel reassured by his tone but was still hoping that they would be married, if not for her sake, then for that of Caroline. She knew Caroline already loved her father. He found it difficult to come to the point. He knew from her infrequent but loving letters that she hoped for them to get together again. After all it was almost ten years since they had last met. Now he was thirty two and had received some money from a rich relative. So only now, by the dictates of English society, was he in a position to marry.

'I have recently achieved some financial stability,' began Wordsworth. 'Through a family debt being repaid, I have inherited three thousand pounds. But there came with that a condition, a suggestion ...' He was hesitating, and now stumbling a bit with his speech.

'Go on – I think I know already that our lives are not going to be conjoined!'

'I could not get out of the arrangement. I would have forfeited much of the inheritance. Then I would have had no money to settle on you or Caroline!' Wordsworth put his tea cup noisily onto his saucer, showing his nervousness.

'I have waited for you – not for money,' said Annette, the tension making her voice louder.

'My dear,' he began, 'I have to tell you that I am to be married.'

Annette put her hand to her mouth as her heart ran cold. 'Married?'

'Yes. It has been arranged.'

'To whom?' Annette's heart was pounding.

'One of my oldest friends, Mary Hutchinson. I was at school with her ...' he tailed off lamely. 'Yes my dear Annette – it was inevitable. I could not visit you in France. As you know, wars and ructions made that impossible. I do not wish to hurt you, my dearest Annette. I know that and say it from the bottom of my heart.' William leaned over and grasped Annette's hand. 'I want never to hurt you. I'm sorry I was not a rich man when I first met you, and I want to make a settlement. That is really why I've come in person,' said William bashfully. 'And of course to see Caroline at last,' he added quickly.

'A settlement?' queried Annette, wondering what this man's romantic poetic letters had really meant. What their affair had really meant to him. A settlement!

At that moment Dorothy and Caroline stepped back into the cottage. William at once stood up. Dorothy immediately joined in the conversation.

'I trust my brother has explained the situation to you, Annette?' Annette nodded bleakly.

'Tonight we stay at the local inn,' Dorothy continued. 'Tomorrow we're going to the bank to complete the necessary paper work. We'll transfer a certain amount of money into your account.'

'Annette, my dear,' interrupted William, 'I want to do the right thing by you and my daughter. I can afford it now – to be regular in the payments. I will instruct the bank to pay to you each month thirty pounds or so.'

Dorothy said, 'That should help you to pay bills.'

Annette could almost hear her add ... 'and quieten your tongue!'

William then stood up and announced that he would take Caroline out for that promised walk.

He later wrote a poem about the shared walk:

It is a beauteous evening, calm and free,
The holy time is quiet as a Nun
Breathless with adoration; the broad sun
Is sinking down in its tranquility;
The gentleness of heaven broods o'er the Sea;
Listen! the mighty Being is awake,
And doth with his eternal motion make
A sound like thunder—everlastingly.
Dear child! dear Girl! that walkest with me here,
If thou appear untouched by solemn thought,
Thy nature is not therefore less divine:
Thou liest in Abraham's bosom all the year;
And worshipp'st at the Temple's inner shrine,
God being with thee when we know it not.

EXTRACT FROM DOROTHY WORDSWORTH'S JOURNAL
SUNDAY AUGUST 1 1802

We arrived at Calais at 4 o'clock on Sunday morning the 31st of July[1 Aug] ... We walked by the sea-shore almost every Evening with Annette & Caroline or Wm & I alone ... seeing far off in the west the Coast of England like a cloud crested with Dover Castle, which was but like the summit of the cloud – the Evening star & the glory of the sky ... Nothing in Romance was ever half so beautiful. Now came in view as the Evening star sank down & the colours of the west faded away the two lights of England, lighted up by Englishmen in our Country to warn vessels of rocks or sands. These we used to see from the Pier when we could see no other distant objects but the Clouds the Sky & the Sea itself. All was dark behind. The town of Calais seemed deserted of the light of heaven, but there was always light, & life, & joy upon the Sea itself. – One night, though, I shall never forget, the day had been very hot, & William & I walked alone together upon the pier – the sea was gloomy for there was a blackness over all the sky except when it was overspread with lightning which often revealed to us a distant vessel. Near us the waves roared & broke against the pier, & as they broke & as they travelled towards us, they were interfused with greenish fiery light.

The more distant sea always black and gloomy. It was, also beautiful on the calm hot nights to see the little Boats row out of the harbour with wings of fire & the sail boats with the fiery track which they cut as they went along & which closed up after them with a hundred thousand sparkles balls shootings, & streams of glowworm night. Caroline was delighted.

On Sunday the 29th of August we left Calais at 12 o'clock in the morning and landed at Dover at 1 on Monday the 30th. I was sick all the way ...

TED'S LIGHT

Lyn McKinney

Ted opened one eye. It was one of those unnaturally bright spring mornings, and he was a long way up. The early light had found its way through the tiny window of his room and was shining directly on his face like a spotlight. He blinked in the unaccustomed glare, rolled over to get his spectacles from the bedside table, coughed and settled back onto the pillows.

There was a tapping at the window. It was the black-headed gull that always greeted him first thing. He would miss that.

Ted swung his weary legs onto the floor and found his slippers. 'All right, young Blackie, I'm coming.' He crossed to the bread bin on the table and pulled out an old crust which he broke up on the windowsill and let the bird in. It nearly filled the entire window frame as it wandered through, its grey and white feathers ruffling in the wind. Then it dipped its beak and snatched a large crumb, letting it roll to the back of its throat, before swallowing it. Ted watched as piece after piece disappeared in the same fashion. 'Where will you get your breakfast tomorrow, old son?' he said to the gull.

The gull looked up at him, its head cocked on one side. Ted reached over and gently stroked the top of its black, feathered head. It stood stock still for him, seeming to enjoy the attention. 'Bye bye Blackie' said Ted. 'Have a good life.' He turned away, and the gull left him to soar in the air draughts outside.

It was time to extinguish the light now dawn had come. Ted slowly climbed the spiral stone steps one by one, feeling the wooden rail with one hand and the cold central wall with the other. He was more out of breath than he'd like to admit when he made the top and opened the Lamp Room door.

Ted never failed to be impressed when he saw the huge Fresnel lens surrounding the light. Last night, just before dusk as always, he had climbed the stairs, turned on the kerosene fuel to the lamp and checked the lens was clean before lighting it. Then he had worked the clockwork gears to make sure the lens was revolving properly. Ted's light shone out across the sea just as it had done for the past ten years. Who knows how many ships might have foundered on the rocks below if his flashing beacon had not been there?

After he stopped the fuel and the gears and the light dimmed, he pulled a clean cloth out of his trouser pocket to polish the lens to perfection. He was determined to leave the old girl in a state of readiness. After all, he was king of his castle. Then, just for a moment, his cleaning complete, he sank gratefully onto the narrow circular bench seat before heading back down to the Watch Room.

Ted traipsed across to the old kitchen cupboard, where he found a tin of corned beef and some baked beans. Pulling out the drawer beneath, his hands felt for the tin opener. He heated the beans on a two-ring gas stove and boiled some water for tea, adding the end of a tin of evaporated milk to his mug when it was brewed. Then he sliced some meat, smiling to himself that it would make a good meal for a condemned man. That's how he felt, as he settled into an old armchair in the Watch Room, balancing the plate on its wide arm.

Larry had left weeks ago, saying he wasn't going to wait for the inevitable, and was now working at the local garage. Ernie had spent his last night with Ted a couple of days previously and then left with his daughter to live in Brighton. It had been a painful parting of old friends. Since then, Ted had been on his own, packing up what small items remained – a library of books, puzzles and games, some odd tins of food and a few work clothes. He'd like to say the whole process had been cathartic but in truth it had felt like the end of everything.

After his breakfast, he took a turn outside. As he opened the door to the gallery, the force of the wind nearly knocked him over. But Ted was used to this and far worse. His gnarled old hands gripped the rail as he walked slowly round, inspecting the view from all points, the wind lifting his greying hair and flapping the collar of his flannel shirt.

Below him, the waves lashed the sunlit rocks unceasingly. He raised his hand to shield his eyes from the sparkle of the sea on the horizon, a gesture that he'd made a thousand times before. A couple of old iron tankers were anchored in the distance, and a lone yacht passed by the point, its triangular sail like a folded pocket handkerchief.

Ted stood drinking in the view, listening to the gulls wheeling overhead and wondered if anywhere else would compare with this. When the three of them had been together, they'd been a tight unit. If one had been on watch, another would be cooking and the third asleep. They'd lived their lives like submariners, often in the dark and the cold, but they'd had the warmth of their conversation and laughter, their comradeship.

Ted had never married, though as a youngster he'd courted a few girls like his mates, before and after he joined the navy. They had all been pretty enough, but then he met Nancy. Unlike the others, she had definitely not been bowled over by his uniform. In fact, she'd tried to avoid him at first, saying all sailors were in love with themselves. By the time they realised they were meant for each other, Ted's leave had run out and Hitler was bombing the southern shipyards. Two days after he returned to his ship she died in a direct hit. After that, no one else measured up somehow.

Ted sighed, remembering the few days they had together. Had she lived, life might have taken a different turn, but he didn't regret his decision to join the lighthouse family. He'd trimmed and lit lamps in over fifteen lighthouses around the country, and his comrades had seen him through thick and thin, in all weathers. They were all of a type, lighthouse keepers. Men who enjoyed their own company. Of course, there was always the odd rogue worker who found the silence deafening, but there hadn't been many of those. And he'd enjoyed looking after the lamp and all its attendant equipment.

He returned to the Watch Room, the heavy gallery door slamming behind him in the wind and crossed to the old desk in the corner. From the top of a pile, he picked up the log book and opened it. Here he and Ernie, and more lately Larry too, had taken it in turns to record the weather and tide times each day, along with the occasional incidents at sea; from the transport of patients from oil tankers by helicopter to the rescue of foolhardy yacht skippers chancing the weather. He picked up a biro and wrote 'AUTOMATION' in large letters against the date, then snapped the book shut, leaving it square in the middle of the desk.

It was nearly time. They would be coming soon. Ted washed up his plate and mug and cutlery, leaving them on a tea towel to dry on the old wooden board, and pulled out his suitcase from under the bed. He sat down to take off his slippers, swapping them for a pair of wellingtons. His all-weather coat hung loosely on the back of the door, waiting for him. After a final look around, he slowly opened the Watch Room door and, suitcase in hand, began his descent over one hundred steps.

Down below, the wind was more of a strong breeze. The sun was warming up the earth nicely. He could see the shoots of vegetables he'd planted earlier in the year just poking through the soil in the keepers' allotment. Ted smelt the salty tang in the air and thought he'd climb down to the water's edge one last time. He dropped his suitcase by the door and worked his way down the steep slope to the top of the rocks, covered in barnacles and still slippery from the last high tide.

When they arrived with their vans full of equipment, there was no sign of Ted. Just a battered old suitcase containing a few clothes and a framed photograph of a pretty brunette and her sailor. Ted's light had finally gone out.

PLEASURE BEACH

Hilary Hanbury

It is a part of my life.
It is loud and brash.
It is where I had my first romance.
It is where I was rescued when I was seventeen,
Borne down a ladder by a fireman, from the broken wheel.

Kneeling on a feather mattress at Nana's,
Digestives, hot milk and honey.
Watching from her window, shrieks from the Waltzer.
And later, teenage and horny
Fairground riders smell of sugar and diesel and sweat
Dark and brooding, older, fags hanging from their beautiful lips.

It is a sadder, shrunken place now,
Once a crowning glory,
The Scenic Railway heading nowhere,
Dwarfed by greater things.
The Giant has moss on his feet.

The Funhouse is no fun anymore.
Penny arcades now fifty pence a go,
And now you have plastic tokens
To ride the ancient gallopers.
My teenage wages condensed into five, three minute rides.

THE CODFATHER – A VIGNETTE

Scott King

The 'Fish Tea' usually happened on a Tuesday. One of the perks of my dad's job as a fishmonger was that every week he was able to bring home a treat for us – some fish from the North Sea. I use the word 'treat' loosely because, looking back, it was hard to tell who it was actually a treat for. Was it a treat for me, who would cry throughout the meal and go to bed hungry, or was it a treat for my parents who were forced to repeat the same old clichés and watch me snot all over the gaff whilst trying to enjoy the evening meal? The smell was actually the first hint of the terror that was upon me. My dad would come in and I'd be in my bedroom watching Thundercats, or some other kids' TV show that you don't get nowadays. My room was off the kitchen; an extension they had built when I got too big to be carried upstairs, on account of my disability. I'd usually just close the door when he came in and I saw him produce the blue bags, (fish from the market, if you don't know, was always wrapped in blue bags for some reason). Sometimes this was in anger but most of the time just in quiet defeat.

Fish. I hated fish. I knew that on Fish Night I would be going to bed hungry. The level of hunger often depended on what the fish was served with. If it was chips, there would be the batter from the fish and the chips to eat so that wasn't too bad but if my mum was feeling super-sadistic it would be new potatoes and peas. The level of trauma depended on the accompaniment.

'Tea time,' Mum would shout. Her voice was different on Fish Night, as if she knew what was coming. She must have hated Fish Night just as much as I did, well not quite as much, that was hardly possible. As I opened my door the smell would hit me, ironically like a proverbial wet kipper. I would sometimes gag, much to my mother's annoyance. I knew when my mum was annoyed because she clicked her tongue … A LOT. We sat at the table, me, my mum, my dad and my sister. My sister never minded fish so her involvement in the whole charade was limited. Week in week out, I did the same thing. I would eat what I liked before the "fun" could really start. Then there was a painful hour of tears, threats and tantrums before the parental unit would crack and I was allowed to leave the table. I was free of fish, for a week at least. Why do kids do that? Why can't they equate that if they eat some of the food they do like at the same time as the stuff they don't, it will taste about 35% better? Obviously it won't be 50/50 because the horrible food has a much stronger taste and that's why we don't like it in the first place.

I don't eat fish now, or any kind of seafood, and it's all because of the trauma I suffered at a young age. I can't walk past any seafood stall or the fish section in the supermarket without holding my breath and if I can take an alternative route, no matter how much longer it takes, I'll take it. As an adult, I feel like I've been robbed of a cuisine that I could have grown to like had it not been for those blue bags of horror. Oh well, where did I put that rib eye?!

NINETEEN

Lyn Hazleton

Amanda

I knew Maxine was pregnant. When she told me, she asked me to keep it to myself, she hadn't told Gavin yet, she was waiting for the right moment. I said I would, but I wasn't comfortable about it and decided to share it with Bill, ask him what he thought. He pulled a face, said he didn't believe it, but if it were true, then we shouldn't get involved. It was their business he said. I reminded him we were walking to the village pub with them later for a drink. I was worried it was going to be awkward. Gavin was our neighbour, had been for over twenty years, but Maxine had only recently moved in with him and, although we liked her, she was a lot younger than us. However, it had been a busy week. I was frazzled, Bill had been working long hours. We needed a night out. Let's enjoy ourselves we said to each other.

The pub was busy when we arrived. We squeezed in and made our way towards the bar chatting to a few of the regulars as we passed. The men queued for drinks, leaving us to find a table. There wasn't one, the place was so full but I spotted two vacant stools at the other end of the bar. Maxine hurried to grab them whilst I mouthed to Bill where we'd be, pointing towards the far wall. When I joined Maxine, she didn't notice me at first, her head was down, tapping on her phone. Then she looked up, shoved her phone in her hand bag and plastered a false smile on her face.

'Not work I hope?' I said.

'No, a friend.'

'Don't let me stop you.' I slipped my jacket off and climbed on the other stool feeling dowdy in my jeans and plain cotton blouse. Maxine wore a black halter-neck dress with a flare at the knee, bottle-green tights and spiky-heel ankle boots. Her straight auburn hair was loose down her back and falling across her bare shoulders.

'You look great,' I said. Her eyes were lined with navy-blue and her cheek bones shone with glitter. When Maxine told me she was pregnant, she glowed. She had the same look about her now. Her skin was flawless with a sprinkling of sandy freckles across her nose. A silver stud sparkled at her left nostril.

Ignoring my compliment, she crossed her long legs and folded her slender arms. She reminded me of a newborn fawn.

'Don't,' she said, a frown puckering her brow, her tea-coloured eyes holding mine. 'Don't look at me like that.'

'Like what?'

'Like you know something.'

I leant towards her, catching her perfume. A dim reminder of patchouli oil floated in my mind.

'But I do know something.' Over her shoulder, I could see Bill and Gavin were heading towards us with the drinks. I quickly changed the subject. Bill passed me a glass of Merlot. I took a gulp, eager for the hit of alcohol. I was glad of the distraction. When we'd clinked our glasses and said cheers, Gavin took up a story, something to do with work. I was content to let the men talk and began to relax, their conversation allowing me to retreat from a difficult situation. Maxine was drinking wine in small steady sips. She fixed her eyes on Gavin, as he and Bill relayed the trials of their week and their commute into London.

They were good friends, Gavin and Bill, shared an interest in motor sport, politics and their work.

'Ten more years and I'm out of it,' Bill said. 'By then Amanda will have a chain of shops and I'll be able to retire.' He winked at me, tipped his head back and drained his beer. Gavin followed his lead, wiping the side of his hand across his lips.

'You two carry on like that and you won't make ten more years,' I said.

Maxine gathered her hair up in both hands and let it fall back across her shoulders. 'In ten years, I'll be forty-six,' she said. 'Yikes, I don't like the sound of that.'

'Ha! You'll still be working and I'll be retired, taking it easy and playing golf.' Gavin laughed, pulling his wallet from the back pocket of his jeans. 'Same again?'

'I can't think of anything more boring.' Maxine finished her wine and handed him her glass.

When he'd headed for the bar, I tried to catch Maxine's eye. I didn't think she should be drinking, but she was smiling breezily, avoiding my stare. She'd become animated. She was telling us some tale about her dad playing golf in Portugal. She was laughing, waving her hands in the air between us. Bill and I exchanged glances. She reminded me of our daughter and I wondered if Bill thought the same. Then I spotted a vacant table with soft seats, our usual place by the open fire and suggested we hurry to take it.

Maxine nudged past me to sit on the sofa, grabbed a cushion, and placed it in the small of her back.

'Sit next to me, Amanda,' she said patting the space beside her. She cosied up to me. 'Girls together,' she giggled. I inched away from her and found myself missing old times when I'd sat on this very sofa with Barbara, Gavin's ex-wife, when all our kids were at home. I still thought about Barbara and wondered why she had an affair. Gavin didn't deserve that. When he met Maxine I was pleased for him but I was concerned when she moved in so quickly and I did wonder what she saw in a man who was nearly twenty years older than her. When Gavin told us she was only thirty six, I remember saying to Bill, it wasn't going to last, not unless Gavin was prepared to change and I doubted that was possible. Maxine was single and I had it in my mind she'd be pleading with him for a baby. When she told me she was pregnant, I tried to remain impassive, despite her barrage of questions. I kept my concerns to myself. I had a very good idea what Gavin's reaction would be when he found out.

When Gavin returned with the drinks, I looked at her over the rim of my glass and shook my head. She leaned towards me, put her mouth to my ear and told me not to be a mother hen. That did it for me. It was her life, her baby, her choice. It really was none of my business.

I had all but forgotten the conversation I'd had with Maxine that morning when the call for last orders came. Bill went up to the bar to get them in, so it was just me, Maxine and Gavin left at the table. It was very hot in the pub and I could feel the heat of Maxine's body leaning against me. She became very subdued, resting her head on my shoulder, putting the flat of her hand against her belly and stroking it.

'You OK Maxine?' I said.

'No, not really,' she said. She stood up, felt her way around the table and dropped herself into Gavin's lap. She draped her arms around him and nuzzled into his neck. Gavin looked at me and frowned. I should have said something then. Instead I excused myself. I sensed something was going to blow up and I didn't want to be brought into it.

In the ladies I stalled for time. I brushed my hair, tidied my makeup and chatted to a girl in one of the cubicles. When I went back to our table, Gavin and Bill were engrossed in a conversation but there was no Maxine. It was closing time; the bar had thinned. 'Where's Maxine?' I said.

'She's gone.' Gavin reached for his glass, took a slug of his beer. There was a dark sweat circle staining his shirt under his armpit. He raked a hand through his hair.

'Go after her then, catch her up.' We only lived minutes away, but the lane was dark and pot-holed. I grabbed hold of his sleeve and tugged at it.

Bill threw me a warning glance but I ignored him.

'Get after her Gavin, she might not be well. If you don't, I will.'

'Fuck it!' He whipped his jacket from the back of his chair and stormed out of the pub.

Maxine

I could tell Amanda was uneasy the moment we got into the pub. I felt her stare, the urgent look in her eye. She wanted to pass me a silent message. I was beginning to wish I hadn't told her I was pregnant, but I hadn't stopped to think. When the blue lines appeared on the tester, my whole insides seemed to disappear to be replaced by a gaping, yawning hole. I shoved the stick into the back pocket of my jeans and rushed next door. I needed to tell someone and I hoped Amanda would give me some insight into what

I could expect when I told Gavin, but I'd miscalculated. I should have realised where her loyalty lay.

At the pub, what I didn't expect was for her to go all serious on me. I was beginning to feel judged, so when I took the wine from Gavin, I turned away from her and pretended I was interested in the conversation he was having with Bill, but there was tedium to it and I soon felt bored. All I could think about was this thing I'd allowed to happen. I knew I'd been taking risks, sleeping with Craig, but I felt I needed time to work out where I stood with Gavin before cutting ties. It was a mess and I hated myself for it.

The chatting droned on and, as I sipped my wine, I allowed myself to drop into a fantasy: Gavin would be ecstatic about the baby. He would sweep me away to some exotic island in the Indian Ocean to celebrate. While we were there he would ask me to marry him. The wedding would be small; I'd wear a simple shift dress in lemon silk. My hair would be secured in a high bun with tendrils falling about my face. The baby would be born. A girl. We would call her ... hmm, what would I choose? I daydreamed endlessly about girl's names until finally I noticed I'd finished my wine, Gavin was at the bar getting refills and Amanda and Bill were heading for a table by the fire.

Once we'd settled down, I remember thinking this was better. It was as if I'd found my way out of the fog. The wine had hit me and I'd begun to enjoy myself. I'd developed a love for intoxication, for the numbing sensation it gave me and I wanted that feeling. Gavin knew it well. He liked this part of me. It reminded him of his youth I guess. I caught his eye and he winked at me. I liked the intimacy. He was an attractive man. There was something about the silver in his hair and the lines around his eyes. His face was worn, like a fisherman's. He was earthy, rugged. My sort of guy. I smiled back at him and took up the banter. I talked an awful lot from then on. I gesticulated wildly too and as the evening went on, the hubbub of laughter and people talking in the pub meant I needed to shout to be heard. I must have worn myself out, because when the call for last orders came, I'd had enough. I flaked out against Amanda, my hand resting on my belly. It was warm beneath the satin of my dress. I wanted Gavin to feel it too. I went and sat on his lap, nuzzled up close and kissed him. The evening was over. I wanted to get out of the pub, to get him alone.

'It's late,' I murmured in his ear. 'Let's go.'

'Bill's getting the last round in, we can't.'

'Yes we can.' I kissed him again, more insistent this time.

'No Maxine.' He pulled my arms away from around his neck and pushed me off his lap.

'Gavin, I need to talk to you. Alone.' I leaned towards him.

'What about?'

'It's private, not in here. I need you to listen to me.'

'Can't it wait until we get home? I'll listen to you then.'

'Bullshit you will,' I said loudly, momentarily forgetting the other people sat at the tables around us. 'You never want to listen to me!'

He got defensive, angry. He said yes, all right, he didn't want to listen to me. He accused me of wittering on about rubbish all the time, embarrassing him in front of his friends, whining about the hours he kept at work, how the house still had his ex-wife's smell in it, that I wanted us to move and he didn't. That he was losing his sense of what he wanted. He ended his speech with the words: 'I didn't think it would be this way.'

That said it all. I gathered up my bag and coat and headed for the door, bumping into to people, not caring I'd made a scene.

Gavin

I was angry. She'd spoilt the night. I was embarrassed too. Embarrassed she'd behaved like a petulant teenager. I was pretty much embarrassed about myself as well. Bill had tried to warn me numerous times before, but it wasn't until that night I'd begun to take proper notice. When Maxine stormed out of the pub, let her go, I thought. Bill came back with the drinks then. When I told him what had just happened, he laid into me with the truth.

'She's nineteen years younger than you, Gavin. Christ, look at you man, you're going grey, your kids are having kids, you've given up squash to play golf and you're planning retirement. Think about it! You're in a mid-life crisis and you need to do something about it. Fast. Before ... well hell, I'll say it ... before you get trapped.'

'OK, I get it, I'm old, I'm past it.' I thought he'd make a joke then, we'd have a laugh, finish our beer and call it a night, but he sat down next to me, made me look at him and reeled off a string of reasons why I needed to consider what I was doing. He said more stuff about men and the mid-life crisis, all the clichés came out. It stung, I have to say, but the truth does, right? It's difficult to explain exactly what I felt but I could feel a fear rising in me. What was I doing? All I wanted in that moment was to have things back as they were, to have my wife with me again. Bill was still going on. I dropped my head down, elbows on my knees. I'd stopped listening. My eyes were smarting. Amanda returned from the ladies. Her arrival, her concern for Maxine didn't alter the situation. I knew what I was going to do.

I left the lights of the pub behind me and hurried along the dark lane, cursing I'd forgotten to bring a torch. The brambles of the hedgerow snagged against my jacket. My boots scuffed the gravel as I broke into a jog. Nineteen. Nineteen years. Christ, get a grip you fool. At the end of the lane, I turned the corner, stumbled into the verge and nearly lost my footing. I was sweating, cursing under my breath, then I saw her in the glow of our security light.

'Maxine,' I yelled as she reached the gate. She stopped, turned around.

'It's you,' she said.

'Who else?'

She opened the gate, walked down the path. Her door keys rattled as she took them out of her pocket.

'Maxine, we need to talk.' I reached out and put my hand on her shoulder.

'That's exactly what I said to you.' She spun around to face me, her eyes flaring.

'Ok, come on then. Let's do it. Inside though.' I tried to nudge her towards the door, but her body was rigid.

'No. Here. Let's say it here. You didn't think it would be this way, you said, back in the pub. Nor did I. I didn't think it would be this way, but it is.' She faltered ... took a breath. 'Gavin ... I'm pregnant.'

After she'd said it, she slumped against me, her head heavy against my chest. I had an almighty urge to throw her off, push her away from me, but I stood there. I felt heavy, static, like I'd grown roots. My mind turned to pulp. My stomach clenched and I felt sick, the beer rising up at the back of my throat.

'Gavin, say something.'

I disentangled myself from her and stepped back. I put my arms out, palms facing forward.

'If you are, it's not mine. It's not possible.' I backed away from her. 'This has been a big mistake. My keys, give me my keys.'

COFFEE AT RYAN'S

Rupert Mallin

we meet
        each end of a Sutton Park seat
      we smile
my left eye lazy

and the day unwinds like a sheet
     of balances
         I can't complete

coffee at Ryan's beckons
      it's on the corner of Dale Street
         in our closed community

I know I smell of an old wardrobe
      head to toe
and that you will pay my way:
      bonbon biscuits
        and a Latté

you dress neat
      and smell of lavender
and the veins on your hands are narrow roads
      I took you down in 1968
        to fields of wheat
           and Chiltern Stream

we hid in a railway hut from the sleet
      and I was so shy
        I stood in the doorway
my back a sheet
     of ice

you hold out your hand across the Formica
      as if I'm invited home
        but I retreat
as I've always done

      and we look out at the sunshine
      and your goodbye
        is my defeat

BIOGRAPHIES

The Norwich Forum Writers

In 2012, Norwich became England's first UNESCO City of Literature. This success created a buzz amongst both experienced and aspiring local writers. In 2014, a creative writing initiative began within the Norfolk & Norwich Millennium Library, located at The Forum. From the beginning, the ethos of the group was, and remains, one of inclusivity.

Norwich Forum Writers is volunteer-led, with fortnightly meetings taking place on a Friday morning from 10.30 until 12:00. Participation is free and we welcome anyone interested in creative writing to join us within the relaxed, open and friendly environment of the Millennium Library.

Our programme of meetings runs from September to July and is designed to incorporate a wide range of topics and themes. Participants are given the opportunity to do some writing and are encouraged to share their ideas and experiences. All of the group activities are voluntary; there is no pressure to write or join in, just listening and observing others is welcomed.

If you have ever wondered if you can write, here is a safe, encouraging and free way to find out. We look forward to meeting you.

Linda Ford - Linda is a retired primary school teacher who has loved sharing writing and books with her children and grandchildren. On her retirement, she took two creative writing courses and one children's writing course at the University of East Anglia. Since joining Norwich Forum Writers, Linda has begun to explore the exciting but challenging world of adult fiction and poetry. Editing and redrafting work has given her the passion to develop her many ideas into completed stories and she now finds she can't stop writing.

Hilary Hanbury - Hilary was born in Norfolk, raised in Suffolk, flitting around the country before returning to her birthplace. She is passionate about writing and has had work published in an anthology about women in rural Norfolk. When she was ten she won a national writing competition receiving a certificate and a year's supply of Cadbury's chocolate. She writes poetry and fiction and is completing her first novel spanning eight decades and says it feels like it has taken that long to write it.

Peter Hardinge - Peter's creative background ventured him into Norwich Forum Writers as a progression from his love of both the arts and sciences, coupled also with a need to fill time in semi-retirement! He has always enjoyed creative writing, reading, cooking and gardening and balancing daily life with working from home and in London. Amateur stage perform-ances helped him at a young age to appreciate fulfilment of the arts as did his love of literature and painting.

Lyn Hazleton - Lyn's career brought her to Norwich in 1997 to work for Aviva. When her role as IT Project Manager was made redundant, she retrained as a psychotherapist. With an interest in writing for personal therapy, in 2014 she attended a creative writing course where she completed her first short story. Lyn has been writing ever since. She appreciates the wealth of literary activities available in Norwich and is currently exploring creative non-fiction.

Kathryn B Hollingworth - Kathryn grew up in the Derbyshire Peak District and started to write poems when she was nine, several of which were published by the Sheffield Star. She moved to Norwich in 1995 and has completed certificated courses in writing crime fiction and historical fiction at UEA. Recently she has self-published two supernatural fiction books. She loves being part of Norwich Forum Writers and finds the topics covered very interesting.

Shirley Valentine Jones - Shirley's first job was at the University of London Press, London, with Sir David Attenborough who was then just a young man. She became a reporter for Ruislip Weekly Press newspapers and continued to be a journalist in Canada and an Assistant Editor on the Kodiak Weekly news in Alaska in 1957. In her late twenties, she went to teachers' training college and taught English until retiring in 1997. She loves writing short stories and poems, and is now trying to write her first novel.

Scott King - Scott has lived in Norwich for ten years, having been born and raised in the ever-so-sleepy town of Lowestoft. He enjoys the cinema, theatre, music and, of course, writing, He writes short stories and flash fiction, some of which are based on real life experiences. His writing style is often sardonic, self-deprecating and witty.

Lyn McKinney - Lyn was a broadcast journalist and arts reviewer for BBC East before she retired. She is keen to write creatively, having written news for many years. A little of her work was published in 'Gullstones and Cuckoos' three years ago and, as well as writing, she loves to paint and watch good theatre. She lives south of Norwich with her husband, and golden retriever Harry.

Phil McSweeney - Phil simply enjoys creative writing, learning the craft of it, and hopefully giving pleasure to others. He concentrates on writing fiction for children and young adults. He writes with great humour and imagination. He has several picture books, a children's chapter book and one and a half novels on a laptop somewhere. He would like to count publishers among his friends but that has not yet come to pass.

Rupert Mallin - Over four hundred of Rupert's poems were published in magazines and books from 1973 to 2005 - Poetry Review, Ambit, Tribune, Redbeck Press, etc. He also had plays performed in theatre and two have been broadcast on BBC Radio 4. However, writing left him for over a decade. Norwich Forum Writers has enabled him to return to writing with renewed enthusiasm.

Mary Maynes - Imogen has lived in Norwich for many years and is an avid reader. She enjoys all sorts of theatre, both amateur and professional, as well as entertaining her friends and family by telling stories. She has not previously put pen to paper, unless you count the school magazine many years ago. Norwich Forum Writers encourages anyone and everyone to have a go; and so she has.

Simon Richardson - Simon is a Norwich man who sees the world through a life-time's experience in writing. It has always been a life lived with pen in hand. It's an ability honed from a working life in Royal Mail. Retirement expanded his desire to write. Simon joined various writing groups with much encouragement at Café Writers and Jurnet Poetry. He is particularly nourished in the Norwich Forum Writers' group. He has also found a niche in local dramatics and script writing.

Anasua Sarkar Roy - Anasua grew up in London, and although she loved to dance as a girl, much of her time was spent reading and writing. She was distracted for twenty years whilst she qualified and worked as a biochemical engineer, accountant and management consultant. Creative writing courses at the University of East Anglia, Cinema City, National Centre for Writing and the Norwich Forum Writers, along with her daily yoga practice, inspired her to write again.

Gill Wilson - Gill has lived in Norwich for many years and loves the vibrancy of the Norwich Forum. Although she has always loved reading, the cinema and visiting both amateur and professional theatres, writing is relatively new to her. She likes to challenge herself by entering stories into competitions in writers' magazines. Flash fiction and short stories are her preferred choices but she has recently discovered the haibun. As a teacher of children who have barriers to learning, she particularly enjoys the inclusive nature of the Norwich Forum Writers.

Sophie Yeomans - Sophie likes writing, she has had a few articles and poems published in the past and feels Norwich Forum Writers can provide an opportunity to develop this capacity.